1

'Surely you remember Russ Stretton?'

Angela wrinkled her nose, pretending to consider the question. She remembered Russ Stretton all too well but it required an Oscar-winning performance to pull the wool over her mother's eyes.

'He's in France, isn't he?' she asked in as casual a voice as she could manage, trying not to recall the embarrassing crush she'd had on Russ when she'd been a gauche teenager.

Angela couldn't forget the lazy blue eyes mocking her attempt at sophistication as she pretended to know all about modern carpentry and the merits of pine against oak.

She had been waiting in the kitchen for her mother to finish her cleaning job at Jacob's Bluff, the Stretton family home, when Russ had ambled through from the cold room, clutching a beer.

The heat was stifling and did nothing to lower Angela's temperature, which had rocketed at the sight of Russ wearing cut-off jeans and a tight white tee shirt. She did her best to disguise the glass of milk she had been drinking and wished she hadn't been wearing her school uniform.

'Mind if I join you?' he asked, as if he was visiting her home.

He'd sat down opposite Angela on the spare kitchen chair and stretched out his long legs.

'What's that you're reading?' he asked.

Angela screwed up her fanzine and thrust it back into her school bag. Russ's eyes had teased hers and Angela knew he had glimpsed the boy band posing on the front.

'Don't mind me,' he said, 'I'm waiting for some glue to dry but in this heat it could be some time.'

'You're a qualified carpenter aren't you?'

'Almost. I'm doing the practical bit

ANGELA'S RETURN HOME

It has been years since school-teacher Angela Banks last saw Russ Stretton, but she remembers him only too well. She'd had a massive crush on him as a teenager, and now he's back in her life. But he's carrying considerable emotional baggage, including a five-year-old son, Mikey — not to mention a sophisticated French ex-wife, who seems intent on winning him back at all costs . . .

MARGARET MOUNSDON

◆

ANGELA'S RETURN HOME

Complete and Unabridged

LINFORD
Leicester

First published in Great Britain in 2014

First Linford Edition
published 2015

A catalogue record for this book is available
from the British Library.

ISBN 978–1–4448–2552–7

F Published by
F. A. Thorpe (Publishing)
Anstey, Leicestershire

Set by Words & Graphics Ltd.
Anstey, Leicestershire
Printed and bound in Great Britain by
T. J. International Ltd., Padstow, Cornwall

This book is printed on acid-free paper

and that involves hands-on experience.'

'What have you been making?' Angela asked.

'It's my first attempt at a chair,' Russ replied, 'but it's not going too well. Do you know anything about wood?'

'We've got a pine kitchen table.'

'Hm,' Russ nodded agreement, 'I think that's the wood I should have used. Still never mind. You learn by experience. At least my chair's a got a leg on each corner and they're all the same height, or rather they were when I started out.'

Pauline Stretton chose that moment to sweep into the kitchen. She frowned at the sight of her son relaxing with Angela.

'Darling, I didn't hear you come up to the house from the studio.'

'Didn't want to disturb you, Ma,' he replied. 'I know you're always busy.'

'I'll get Mrs Banks to make us some tea.'

'That won't be necessary,' Russ insisted. 'I've got my beer and I really do have to get back to my chair. Angela informs me oak should never be used for kitchen furniture.'

'I only said,' Angela blustered, but Pauline Stretton wasn't listening.

'If you've finished your milk, Angela, dear, I think your mother is ready to leave.'

Angela knew a dismissal when she heard it. She gathered up her school bag, crammed her straw hat on her head and tried not to blush as Russ winked at her. That was the day she fell hopelessly in love with him.

'He's back home,' Isobel Banks interrupted her daughter's memories of the past, 'and what's more he's got his five-year-old son with him, Michel, Mikey for short. He's an engaging little boy.'

'What about Judith?' Angela asked, referring to Russ's stunning wife.

'I believe she's still in France.'

Her mother was not one for gossip, especially not about her employer's son, and Angela knew it would be no good asking her why Judith hadn't come to England with her family.

Angela had first met Judith at one of Pauline's summer parties, when she had been drummed into helping pass round the canapés while guests sipped drinks on the lawn. Her heart had plummeted at the sight of Russ, his arm entwined around his beautiful fiancée's waist. They had been gazing into each other's eyes, totally oblivious to the other guests.

Judith was slender, impossibly chic and Angela felt like a hot, over-ripe daisy in the flowered sundress her mother had made for her out of some material Pauline Stretton had discarded. Russ had cast her no more than a casual glance as she'd offered them the tray of nibbles. Her smile had died on her lips as Judith waved her away and Russ appeared not to even recognise her.

Isobel Banks shifted her leg into a more comfortable position.

'This wretched cast is driving me

mad. I can't wait for it to come off then I'm going to have a good long scratch.'

'If you will go dropping frozen legs of lamb onto your foot, you have to pay the consequences,' Angela chided her mother.

'I'm so annoyed with myself. It was such a silly thing to do.' She pouted. 'I hate sitting around doing nothing. Have you any mending?'

'You've sown up all my hems and my buttons are on so tight they can scarcely breathe,' Angela teased.

'If only I knew how to knit,' Isobel sighed, 'but I never could get my head round knit two, purl one.'

The afternoon sunshine cast a weak ray through the rain clouds scudding across the sky.

'The flower beds need attention too.' Isobel glanced through the window. 'It's so frustrating.'

'Only another two weeks to go,' Angela did her best to raise her mother's spirits, 'then you can go back to work, but you must do as the doctor tells you and take things easy.'

'Are you sure you don't mind going up to Jacob's Bluff in my place?'

'Not at all,' Angela replied.

She wasn't sure how she would react to seeing Russ again but they'd both moved on since her teenage crush. She was now a qualified teacher and Russ was father to a young son.

'It is good to have you home again,' Isobel's gentle smile lit up her face, 'even if the circumstances are not ideal.'

After Angela's latest close shave with a variable speed limit, which resulted in three more penalty points being placed on her driving licence, plus an exhaust system that emitted a more than acceptable level of pollution, she decided that the time had come for a parting of the ways with her ancient run-around that sometimes masqueraded as a car. Her friendly garage mechanic had informed her in dismal tones that it was only a matter of time before the car got there first and parted company with her.

'The bodywork needs urgent attention, and it'll probably cost you more money than it's worth to get it back on the road,' he'd told her when she was bewailing to him how close she had come to losing her driving licence.

'I don't speed,' she explained, 'but with the constant road works, the variable limits keep changing. They're never the same from one week to the next and when I'm in a hurry I don't always notice.'

'Could I interest you in a part exchange?' the mechanic suggested. 'I've a very nice little hatchback I could retail at a friendly price.'

It was then Angela made her decision.

'I'm giving up driving.'

The mechanic gaped.

'How are you going to get around? Buses are few and far between and you don't want to be stranded at night in the middle of nowhere. There are parts of town that are quite dangerous,' he said, referring to a new nightclub that had opened up on the outskirts of the industrial estate near to the motorway.

'I'm going home to Norfolk, back to my bicycle.'

She had been back three days now and knew she should never have deserted the salt marshes and the coastline that stretched forever into golden-red sunsets.

An ambitious boyfriend had originally talked her into taking up a teaching position in London.

'We'll have a great time together,' he'd insisted, but after only a month when Angela had hardly seen him at all because he had been working late, he'd taken up with the chairman's personal assistant and that had been the end of their relationship. Angela hadn't been too disappointed. Corporate cocktail parties and being seen in the right places with influential people was not for her.

She had done her best to make friends and people were friendly in the block of flats where she lived but she'd never really settled. Her heart was still in Norfolk.

Although late March was the quiet season, early visitors were starting to arrive. The coastline attracted vast numbers of bird watchers and anglers and an enthusiastic yachting crowd.

Her mother had been delighted to welcome her home, especially after her mobility was impeded when she cracked a bone in her foot. Angela's bicycle had been unearthed from the back of the tool shed and given a thorough once-over. Oil was squirted on the wheel spokes, the chain tightened and the saddle adjusted before she announced it good as new. Her feet itched to work the pedals again. She couldn't wait to explore the sand dunes and re-visit the famed seal colony.

'There's not much night life around here, darling.' Isobel looked hard at her daughter.

'I've never been much of a one for loud music and glitter balls,' Angela

10

replied, recalling how her colleagues had given up trying to get her to go to all-night parties.

'I love having you home but it's not right that you should tuck yourself away. I'm sure I could manage with a bit of help from the neighbours. You should be off somewhere doing the things young people do.'

'Nonsense, I love it here,' Angela announced. 'There's nothing like a Norfolk breeze to blow away the cobwebs.'

'That may be true, but you should be thinking about your future.'

'I am and I'll start looking round for another job as soon as I can. People always want supply teachers.'

'What about a husband and children?'

Angela raised her eyes in exasperation.

'For goodness sake, Mum, stop being so last century. I am only twenty-five, there's plenty of time for that sort of thing.'

'I was married at your age.'

'You had Dad.' Angela softened her voice. 'And anyone would have been a fool to let such a man slip through their fingers but until I find his equal I'll stick to my career.'

'You won't find someone as wonderful as your father if you're stuck at Wagstaffs with me.'

Wagstaffs was the family cottage and the only home Angela had known. Her parents had moved there after a whirlwind courtship when they had met and married within the space of six months. Space was cramped but even after Angela was born they had never seen any reason to move. Isobel had been widowed four years ago but she had decided to stay on and was now settled into a new life, cooking and baking for a variety of clients, as well as helping out at Jacob's Bluff.

'Back to business,' Angela said firmly. 'When does The Honourable Pauline want me to descend on Jacob's Bluff?'

'You shouldn't call her that.' Despite

her admonishing frown Isobel laughed. 'She's actually quite kind.'

'Until she remembers her husband's family was related to the High Sheriff.'

Like Isobel, Pauline was widowed. She and her husband had been very active on the local social scene. Brian's business experience had proved invaluable to the community and Pauline was an excellent hostess and very generous with her time.

Jacob's Bluff was a fine manor house. Pauline had lived there all her married life and she saw no reason to move.

'She still does a fair amount of entertaining and you know how I love to cook,' Isobel insisted. 'Pauline is chair of the ladies' club and her gardens are always open every summer. Then there's the children's charity and the flower club and the fundraisers.'

'I hope Pauline's remuneration reflects all the extra work you do and that you get credit for the hours you put in.'

'You never used to be so mercenary,

darling.' Isobel frowned at her daughter.

'It's working in the smoke that does it.'

'Then I have to say I am glad you're back.'

'Me too,' Angela agreed.

'Of course now Russ is home, with Mikey,' Isobel said, 'I suppose there will be more calls on my time. Two extra males about the place make more work.'

'Is the move permanent?' Angela asked.

'I really couldn't say,' Isobel replied. 'Pauline didn't tell me and I didn't ask.'

'Meaning, it's none of your business, Angela?' her daughter responded with a light smile.

'That's exactly what I mean. Now,' Isobel's tone was brisk, 'I suggest you present yourself at Jacob's Bluff tomorrow morning about nine o'clock. An agency has done some cleaning in my absence but Pauline wasn't too happy with the standard of their work.'

'I'm sure she wasn't,' Angela agreed.

'You may find the place is a bit dusty and the brasses will probably need a good polish.'

'Yes, my lady.' Angela tugged at an imaginary forelock. 'Will it be all right if I use the front door or would the tradesmen's entrance be more suitable?'

'I do actually go round the back,' Isobel admitted, 'but only because all my stuff is in the little store room that leads off the kitchen,' she hastened to add, seeing the light of fire in her daughter's eye. 'Some days Pauline doesn't bother to unlock the front door if she's not expecting visitors.'

'I bet Russ and Cissie use the front door.'

'Seeing as Russ's sister is in New Zealand I shouldn't think Cissie uses either door, now stop all this nonsense and give me a bowl and some eggs. At least I can manage to beat up an omelette for lunch.'

Realising the conversation was at an end, Angela slid off the window seat and went in search of the eggs.

2

Jacob's Bluff was very different from Isobel and Angela's cosy cottage.

Wagstaffs was once farmhands' accommodation, with a view of golden sand at the front. At night as a child Angela would snuggle into her duvet safe in her cosy bedroom under the eaves and listen to the swish of the waves lapping the shore, the gentle sound lulling her to sleep.

In contrast Jacob's Bluff was an imposing mid-19th-century house built on a bluff overlooking a cove that during the summer months swarmed with armies of bird watchers and boat loads of visitors, cameras at the ready, all anxious to catch a glimpse of the basking seals.

Angela could remember playing with Russ's sister Cecily, whom everyone called Cissie. They would explore the coastline together, coming home when driven by hunger or the light fading from the day. In the winter when it was too cold to venture outside they would curl up in front of an open fire and tell each other blood-curdling tales of shipwrecks, pirates and ghosts.

Russ would occasionally join them until at the age of eleven he was sent off to boarding school. His father was frequently away from home and insisted that now Russ was growing up he needed stimulating male company. Pauline had protested but she came from a generation that bowed to a husband's wishes and Russ was duly dispatched to a school on the outskirts of Cambridge.

After that he only came home during the holidays and from then on Angela had seen little more of Russ apart from one long hot summer over which she now preferred to draw a veil.

As she and Cissie grew up it was inevitable that their lives too should go in different directions. They left school and while Angela trained as a teacher Cissie took up nursing, moved to New Zealand and married a sheep farmer.

With these memories going through her mind Angela pedalled along the coastal path, enjoying the feel of the early spring sunshine on her face. The air smelt fresher and cleaner in this part of the world. She wobbled over the uneven surface and put out a hand to steady her basket. It was crammed full of spotless overalls, an apron and a pair of sturdy shoes.

'Surely I won't need all this,' she had protested to her mother.

'Mrs Stretton is very particular that I look my best. I occasionally have to answer the front door to visitors.'

'And we don't want the staff looking a mess do we?' Angela remarked, adding, 'Not that you ever do.'

A frown creased her mother's brow.

'I do hope you're not going to upset Pauline Stretton.'

'Would I ever?' Angela couldn't resist teasing.

'You can at times be rather outspoken.'

'It's OK, Mum, I know you like working at Jacob's Bluff. I won't ruin things for you but,' she added, 'neither am I going to let Pauline Stretton walk all over me.'

'She would never do that.'

Angela wasn't so sure.

'I don't intend giving her the chance,' she replied.

Making sure her mother had everything she needed for the morning, Angela kissed her goodbye then set off for Jacob's Bluff. She was early and decided to take the long way round. The rhythmic action of steady pedalling helped her set her thoughts in order. How would she feel about seeing Russ again? He probably wouldn't even remember her, besides which if what her mother told her was true, he would have his hands full looking after a young son.

Despite Isobel's advice that his personal life was none of her business, Angela couldn't help wondering what

19

had happened between him and Judith.

Angela began the ascent up the incline leading to Jacob's Bluff. Isobel Banks had been cleaning for Pauline Stretton for many years and the relationship between the two women had developed into one of trust and mutual respect, although at times Angela felt Mrs Stretton relied too heavily on Isobel for support when she was entertaining or holding one of her numerous fundraisers. Isobel was an accomplished cook and could never say no to anyone when asked to help out. Angela suspected tiredness had been the reason her mother had dropped the leg of lamb on her foot and she intended to make sure Mrs Stretton was aware of this.

Angela freewheeled down the drive to the house, lifting her feet off the pedals, a smile of pure pleasure on her face. It had been years since she had indulged in such a childish activity and it was still as much fun as ever. In a spirit of devilment she sprayed gravel on the grass as she skidded to a halt outside the imposing facade of Jacob's Bluff, then announced her arrival by enthusiastically ringing her bicycle bell. The stone lions flanking the portals had a look of disapproval on their faces as they all waited for someone to open the door.

Angela's finger hovered over the bell push when an impeccably dressed Pauline Stretton answered the door. She eyed Angela up and down.

'Hello, Mrs Stretton, you look very smart, are you going out?' Angela greeted her, thinking all she needed was a hat and she'd be ready for a society wedding.

'In future I would prefer it if you used the kitchen door when you arrive,' was the reply.

Angela's smile of welcome froze. It looked like they were off to a bad start. She tossed back her shoulder-length auburn hair, the light of battle in her hazel eyes. If they were going to have a confrontation it would be best to get it over with right now.

'The front door is more convenient.'

'For you maybe, but not for me.' Angela's confidence slipped as Pauline continued, 'These days I find walking through from the lounge and down the hall takes me longer than it used to.'

'I didn't realise,' Angela blustered but Pauline silenced her by holding up a hand, quelling Angela's apology.

'If you look in that bundle in your basket, you'll find there's a spare key to the kitchen door so if no one's here, you'll be able to let yourself in. Your mother and I find it's a convenient arrangement that works well for both of us and I see no reason to change it, do you?'

Angela lowered her eyes to her basket. Wrapped up in an apron, there was indeed a large old-fashioned key.

'Is this it?' She held it up.

'Try not to lose it, dear, it would be so inconvenient to have another one cut,' was Mrs Stretton's parting shot as the front door was gently but firmly closed in her face.

Angela's sympathy for the older woman's mobility problems immediately evaporated.

'Round one to Ma, wouldn't you say?' A warm voice in her ear made her jump.

Angela spun round. Russ was standing behind her, a look of amusement on his face. He was taller than she remembered and had filled out a bit since she had last seen him. The years had added maturity to his face. His hair she noticed was in need of a cut and his blue jumper was covered in wood shavings that gave off a sawdust smell.

'Here, let me help you.'

Russ grasped Angela's handlebars and turned the bicycle around before she could protest.

'In case you've forgotten, the kitchen's this way.'

With cheeks still flaming from her encounter with his mother, Angela trailed behind him. Jacob's Bluff was a large house and she should have remembered how far it was from the lounge to the front door and that like her mother Mrs Stretton was not as young as she used to be.

'I'm sorry,' she began.

'What for?' Russ turned puzzled eyes in her direction.

'I was rude to your mother.'

'No you weren't.' Russ surprised Angela by adding, 'You were both setting your boundaries.'

'What does that mean?' Angela demanded.

'It's a generation thing. You don't want to be treated like a maidservant but my mother is anxious to keep up appearances. Your mother uses the back door and Ma is keen to keep up the tradition. Why don't you play along with her rules for the time being and save the angst for something really important? Ma would rather die than let you know that on bad days she walks with a stick.'

Another wash of shame flushed over Angela.

'I didn't know. I shouldn't have said what I did.'

'Don't you be fooled by my mother, she enjoyed the encounter. She doesn't want to be treated any differently because of occasional twinges in her hip. She loves a sparring partner and you're well up to her level I'd say. The two of you are going to get on like a house on fire, you see. Now we've got all that out the way, it's good to see you again.' Russ smiled the lazy smile that Angela remembered. It had set her fingertips tingling when she'd been fifteen years old, he had been eighteen and Angela had had her massive crush on him.

'You're back from France?' Angela asked, anxious to change the subject.

'Yes,' was the muffled reply from inside the tool shed. 'Your bike will be quite safe in here,' he said. 'Although it doesn't look like rain, it's best to keep the saddle under cover. We've had a lot of trouble with pigeons nesting under the eaves and they're not fussy where they deposit their evidence if you get my meaning.'

The kitchen was much as Angela remembered it, large, airy and warm.

'We should have cleared away the breakfast things.' The remains of toast and marmalade were still on the table. 'Only Mikey was in a hurry to explore.'

'Mikey's your son isn't he?'

'Yes. He's five. Coffee?'

'I should be getting down to work.'

'If you clear the breakfast things while I boil the kettle that'll do for a start.'

Tying one of her mother's aprons round her waist, Angela began wiping down the table and squirting washing-up liquid into a bowl, piled high with crockery and glasses.

'We never seem to get round to doing the dishes,' Russ said, 'what with Ma's leg and my work in the studio.'

'You're still a carpenter?' Angela remembered some of the wooden animals he had carved for a Christmas fair Pauline had hosted two years ago.

Angela had intended to buy one as a present to herself but by the time she had finished totting up the proceeds from the raffle, they had all been sold.

'I'm busy setting up a new workshop yes, re-establishing contacts, that sort of thing.'

Russ poured out two mugs of steaming coffee.

'Then your move back home is permanent?'

Russ waited a moment before replying.

'My plans are fluid.'

'I wasn't prying,' Angela began to explain before the back door crashed open and a small boy hurtled into the kitchen with whirlwind speed.

'Papa,' he began, then ground to a halt as his brown eyes registered Angela's presence.

There was no mistaking his resemblance to his mother. Russ's son had the same brown eyes as Judith and he had inherited her colouring, thick, dark hair and Mediterranean complexion.

He sidled up to his father, his eyes never leaving Angela's face.

'Mikey, say hello to Miss Banks,' Russ said.

'*Bonjour*, Mademoiselle Banks,' Mikey mumbled.

'It's polite to address her in English,' Russ insisted.

'Good morning,' Mikey addressed his words to the kitchen floor as he traced a pattern with his foot.

'You can call me Angela,' she offered. She had often encountered bashful body language from some of her less confident pupils.

Mikey threw her a shy smile.

'*Merci.*'

'I thought I heard voices.' There was a strong fragrance of lily of the valley as Pauline Stretton swept into the kitchen.

'*Grandmère.*' Mikey catapulted towards her.

His grandmother's face softened as she bent down to give him a hug.

'What have you been up to now, young man?' she asked, smoothing a recalcitrant lock of hair off his forehead.

'I've been exploring,' he announced.

'You shouldn't go off on your own,' Pauline insisted.

'There's no one to play with me,' Mikey replied, a petulant wobble to his lower lip.

'Tell you what,' Russ leaned forward towards his son, 'why don't we invite Angela to tea? I'm sure we've got some of Isobel's scones somewhere and you've got a stock of jam and stuff, Ma, haven't you? Let's have a party.'

Pauline hesitated. 'I'm not sure it's convenient.'

'And I don't like to leave my mother alone all day,' Angela picked up her cue.

'Make it lunch then.' Russ seemed in no mood to be thwarted. 'Good idea?' he asked his son.

'Yay.'

Angela watched Mikey dance a little jig. His jerky movements indicated he wasn't much used to dancing and his rather formal clothes — long black trousers, white shirt and black lace-up shoes — indicated an indoor lifestyle.

'Jam for lunch?' Mikey stopped dancing as the reality of the situation hit home. 'What would *Maman* say?'

'Your mother isn't here,' Russ insisted, 'and as I am I make the rules.'

Angela glanced at Pauline who now seemed reluctant to look her in the eye.

'I'd better get on,' she said quietly, 'if we're to have a lunch party.'

'Good idea,' Pauline agreed. 'I'm sure I've got one of Isobel's open flans in the fridge. We'll have that as well with some salad.'

Pauline bustled away and Mikey raced off into the garden. Russ got slowly to his feet.

'I'd best be off too. See you later.'

Angela watched him stroll towards his studio workshop above the garage that was once the old coach house. The encounter had more than ever convinced her that things were not right between Russ and Judith.

3

The elegant dark-haired woman sipped her fragrant black coffee. As was the bistro's custom it was piping hot and served in miniscule gold-rimmed white cups. All around her Parisians were taking the opportunity to stroll along the boulevard on the first warm day of spring and enjoy the sunshine.

She put down her cup and inspected the pale white band on the third finger of her left hand. She wasn't sure where her wedding ring was these days. During one of their stormy disagreements she had hurled it at her ex-husband. He'd picked it up off the floor, put it in his pocket and left the apartment without a glance in her direction.

Their divorce had been finalised last week and although it had been amicable Judith was beginning to wonder if she had done the right thing. She had the single life she craved but she was lonely and not sure in which direction to go with her new life.

Things had been so very different when she had lived in England. She'd originally visited the country to improve her knowledge of the language, and when her homesickness had almost become too much to bear a casual acquaintance told her of a vacancy that had arisen for a summer job manning a pleasure boat kiosk on the Norfolk coast. She had leapt at the chance. Norfolk was not a part of the world she knew, but anything was better than London. It was not a capital city she took to. Everywhere was so dirty and everything was so rushed. No one spared the time to stop and talk to each other, especially not to a French girl whose knowledge of the English language was sketchy.

Moving to East Anglia she at first struggled to understand the accent, but she soon settled. The leisurely pace of life was more to her taste. The social scene was active too and not a weekend passed without a beach party, a barbecue or a water sports gala.

It was at a water ski ing rally that she had met Russ Stretton and the attraction had been instant and mutual. He had won first prize in his skills' class that weekend and Judith decided he was the man for her, even if it meant fighting off several local girls, not all of whom took to this French usurper in their midst. Judith hadn't cared. When she put her mind to it there wasn't a man she couldn't charm, and Russ had been amongst their number.

He was different from any other man she had known. He was active and considerate and didn't mind her occasional fits of pique, dismissing them as nothing more than her Mediterranean temperament.

They were married within the year and Mikey was born eleven months later. At the same time Russ's carpentry business began to take off and they settled down to married life. Judith had enjoyed helping Russ with his customer visits and seeing more of the English countryside but after Mikey was born she grew restless. Stuck at home on her own for long periods with only a young baby for company, Judith's homesickness re-emerged and she began to realise that life as a wife and mother was going to be very different from that of a carefree single girl.

Russ's tolerance of her mood swings grew less understanding and they began to argue until Judith threw down the gauntlet. She was no longer prepared to live in England.

The move to France had been a last-ditch attempt to repair their battered marriage but Judith soon discovered that things were not much better in her own country. The nature of Russ's work meant frequent periods apart when he had to go off without her, occasionally to England to complete commissions and attend business meetings, and Judith was lonelier than ever. It wasn't long before Judith again grew restless.

That was when her mother, Madeleine, had stepped in. As a working seamstress she was occasionally able to take Mikey to work with her while Judith set about re-establishing a career. Delighted at last to have something to do, she managed to get a job as an assistant in one of the fashion houses and soon she was back where she belonged, working amongst people she understood, people who spoke her language. Her days were interesting, different and full of all the things she loved — clothes, stimulating conversation with successful people, business receptions and parties.

Anton had entered her life when he had brought his sister into their salon to buy a new outfit for her birthday. Judith had been on the front desk and while his sister had been having her fitting Anton had begun talking to her. She discovered he was a successful artist and part of the bohemian set that frequented the famous Left Bank.

She'd first accepted his invitation for

a viewing of his work in an attempt to make Russ jealous. When things with Anton looked as though they could develop into a more serious relationship Judith's mother intervened.

'This cannot go on,' she had insisted.

'I only act as his hostess,' Judith replied. 'It brings in a little extra money and with Russ away so much, I'm lonely.'

'You are a married woman; you have a husband and a son and no business to be acting as a hostess to a married man.'

Her mother's disclosure had been a body blow.

'Anton's married?'

'You didn't know?' Madeleine Grange raised an eyebrow.

'I don't believe you,' Judith gasped in shock.

'Check it out for yourself.'

A chastened Judith discovered her mother was indeed telling the truth.

'Why all the fuss?' a perplexed Anton challenged her. 'My wife is not here so she will not be upset by our relation-ship, and it's not as if we have done anything to be ashamed of.'

Realising she had been foolish in the extreme, Judith handed in her notice at work and tried her best to act the dutiful housewife, but her days were long and with nothing to do she began to quarrel with Russ.

'My home is in France,' she insisted when Russ explained the reason for his increased absences was because most of his work was in England and perhaps they should consider moving back.

'We could split our time between the two countries,' he reasoned but Judith proved stubborn.

'I will not go back to England. The weather is cold and the food is beyond disgusting. I do not fit in there.'

'You'll have me and with Mikey growing up you'll make friends with the other mothers. My mother will help out if needed and what about all the friends you made when we lived in Norfolk?'

'They belong in the past.'

Judith turned her back on Russ, indicating the conversation was closed.

No amount of argument from him would get her to change her mind. Russ did his best to accept French-based commissions but with his limited knowledge of the language it wasn't easy.

Deciding to surprise her by coming home early one day in time to take Judith out for the afternoon, the telephone had been ringing in the hall of their empty flat as Russ unlocked the door.

'Monsieur Stretton?' a female voice had enquired.

'Yes.'

'I have your son here for one hour now.'

'I'm sorry, who's calling?' Russ demanded.

'Madame Dubois. I run the pre-school group your son attends and your wife has not picked him up yet again.'

'Again?' Russ echoed.

'This is the fourth time in two weeks.

It is not good enough. Madame knows my terms. Mikey must be collected no later than half past two.'

'I'll be right there.' Russ had raced out of the flat to collect a tearful Mikey from play school, where the proprietor had explained she was not prepared to continue with this arrangement. It was a great inconvenience to wait for his wife to turn up and could he please do something about it.

Judith sipped another mouthful of coffee as she recalled the scene that followed between her and Russ. He had not listened to her explanation that she had been trying to find a new job and to her further dismay Madeleine had sided with her son-in-law. The situation had spiralled out of control. Things were said that couldn't be unsaid and quite before Judith knew what had happened the marriage was all but over.

When Russ made plans to return to England, Judith had agreed that Mikey accompany him. Pauline Stretton had offered to look after Mikey and it had seemed a sensible arrangement but Judith hadn't realised quite how much she would miss her son as well as her ex-husband.

She looked up as a shadow fell across the table.

'*Maman.*'

She greeted her mother and the two women kissed.

'To what do I owe the pleasure of this meeting?' Madeleine Grange asked.

'Do I need a reason to have coffee with you?' Judith tempered her question with a light smile.

'No, but we hardly ever do meet up to take coffee together, so what is so special about today?'

Judith knew it was impossible to fool her mother and to pretend otherwise would be an insult to the older woman's intelligence.

'I spoke to Mikey last night via a computer link.'

'How is he getting on?' His French grandmother's eyes warmed at the mention of Mikey.

'He was telling me all about Angela and how much his father likes her and what fun they had eating scones for lunch with his *grandmère* Pauline.'

'And this Angela is?' Madeleine enquired.

'A childhood friend of Russ's sister.'

'And what is she doing at Jacob's Bluff?'

Judith shrugged. 'I think she is the cleaner.'

'What else did Mikey have to say?'

'He says he is beginning to like England and he is learning more of the language every day. His father has made plans for him to attend the local school after Easter.'

A few moments of silence fell between them.

'What do you think I should do?' It was Judith who spoke first.

'You want my advice?' Her mother replaced her coffee cup in its saucer.

'Please.'

'Have you managed to get a job?'

'No one's hiring at the moment. It's

the usual story, the economic situation, my employment history, my references.'

'What is wrong with your references?' Madeleine frowned.

'They're in English. I've tried explaining that my ex-husband is English and that I lived there for a while.'

'And that is a problem?'

'Prospective employers don't think I'm going to stay when I explain that Russ resides in England with my young son.'

'That is a natural assumption for them to make.'

'Do you think I should return to England?'

'Only you can make that decision, chérie, but I would advise you to consider your position carefully. Russ will always be a part of your life as you have a son, however, marriage between the two of you did not work. Moving to England may be a backwards step. On the other hand do you want to remain in France if Russ is determined to stay in England with Mikey?'

'Perhaps I could bring Mikey back to France, then Russ would have to follow him?'

'The child must not be used as a bargaining chip,' Madeleine replied in a firm voice.

'Why should I be the one to change my lifestyle?'

'You don't have to. You agreed to let Russ take Mikey to England. The child is settled there now. You have equal visiting rights and Russ would not deny you access to your son.'

'I know but I would like to persuade Russ to live in France again.'

'Then you have a problem and the longer you leave it the harder it will be to resolve.'

Judith's mother was an astute woman and her daughter liked to talk things through with her.

'So a childhood friend has re-appeared on the scene?' Madeleine changed the subject. 'Do you know her?'

'I have met her once or twice. From what I can remember she was a quiet little thing, not Russ's type at all.'

'She may be all those things,' Madeleine acknowledged, 'but she and Russ share the same history.'

Judith's dark eyes narrowed as she remembered the party where she had first encountered Angela. She had been plump and wearing a schoolgirl-type dress and it was obvious she was madly in love with Russ.

'A word of warning,' Madeleine cautioned, 'if you do decide to visit England remember this time it is not only your happiness at stake. You must not be selfish. You must do what is right for everybody.'

'I know that, *Maman*, but I miss my son. It is two months since I have seen him.'

'Of course,' Madeleine stood up, 'that I understand but you have decisions to make.'

Mother and daughter air-kissed.

'*Au revoir, chérie.*'

Judith watched her mother walk down the boulevard, the sunshine playing on the highlighted streaks of her hair. Although she was in her fifties Madeleine Grange was still capable of turning male heads. Judith wished she had her mother's sense of style and confidence. She clenched her hands. Life without a husband or partner was at times inconvenient, a situation she had not envisaged.

She paid the bill then headed off in the direction of the Gare du Nord. It would do no harm to enquire about the frequency of the connections to England.

4

'Thank you, Jack.' Isobel logged off as Jack Brewer watched her with an approving eye.

'You're coming along great guns, Isobel. We'll soon have you tweeting.'

'I don't need social networking sites, thank you. All I want to know,' Isobel insisted, 'is how to email and to order my catering supplies online.'

'All of which you can now do with ease,' Jack replied. 'There's nothing more I can teach you. I would have shown you before now but you haven't been an easy to pupil to pin down.'

'I should have cracked my toe earlier,' Isobel laughed.

'You don't sit still long enough to switch on a computer,' Jack agreed, 'and that's been your problem. Do you have any more questions?'

'None about computing, but would

you like some coffee before you go? I could do with some refreshment after all that logging in and out and creating new passwords.'

'I'll get it. I don't suppose you've had time to make any of your famous scones?' he asked, raising his eyebrows hopefully.

'Angela defrosted a batch from the freezer last night. You'll find them on the shelf in the pantry.'

'I'd heard Angela was back. How is she?' Jack called through from the kitchen.

'She's taken over my job at Jacob's Bluff until I'm up and running again.'

'Is she home for good?'

'For the moment.'

'I also heard she had given up driving.'

'She found it too expensive to run a car so she's using her bicycle for the moment.'

'I'll look forward to catching up with her.'

'At the moment she's biking up to

Jacob's Bluff every morning. I hope I'll be able to take over from her in a week or so.'

'Did you know Russ Stretton is back as well?' Jack asked.

'How did you find out?'

'He dropped by the garage to see about a new vehicle for his business. He's using his mother's car but it's not really suitable and he needs his own transport. I said I'd look out for something for him.'

Jack spooned coffee into two mugs and put some scones on a plate then carried the tray through to the alcove.

'I should be waiting on you.' Isobel watched him unload the tray and sort out plates and a jar of home-made raspberry jam.

'You mean it isn't a man's place to wait on a woman? Don't let the sisterhood hear you.'

'It's got nothing to do with equality of the sexes. I'm the hostess and it's nothing more than good manners,' Isobel began, then bit her lip as she caught the twinkle in Jack's eye.

'You.' She shook her head in mild exasperation.

'Sorry, didn't mean to tease,' Jack apologised. 'There you go.' He passed over her scone and one of the mugs of coffee.

'I shall be putting on weight,' Isobel complained, 'from the amount of scones I've been eating and the lack of exercise.'

'You'll work it off once you're up and about.' Jack smeared jam on his scone. 'I've never known such a whirlwind as you.'

'There's always so much to do, baking and cooking. Pauline Stretton has put her fundraisers on hold for the moment but there'll be lots to do once we both get back in action.'

'Talking of the Strettons I thought Russ was settled in France.'

Isobel nibbled at her scone. 'I don't know about that but he's got his son Mikey with him, he's a lovely little boy.'

'But not Judith?' Jack raised an eyebrow.

Isobel patted crumbs from her lips with a paper napkin.

'No.'

Jack looked as though he were about to say more on the subject but before he could speak the telephone began to ring.

'Would you answer it for me?' Isobel asked. 'I won't be able to hobble over in time.'

Jack reached the telephone in two strides.

'Hello?' he said, picking up the receiver.

'Jack?' a puzzled voice queried.

'Angela, hi.'

'Did I call your garage by mistake? I meant to ring my mother.'

'I'm at Wagstaffs with your mother. We've just had a session online and I'm pleased to tell you, Isobel is now completely computer literate. Would you like to speak to her? I expect I can help her to the telephone.'

'No, don't disturb her. I called to say I might be late back so we'll have to put lunch on hold. I'm up at Jacob's Bluff but I've discovered a puncture in my bicycle tyre. It'll take me a while to mend it. Russ says there's a repair kit somewhere about the place but he's not sure exactly where.'

'No worries. I'm just about finished up here I'll come and get you. I'll mend your tyre too. We can put your bike in the boot and don't worry about Isobel fainting from lack of food. She's been scoffing scones and drinking coffee all morning so she won't go hungry.'

'Jack,' Isobel protested with a reluctant smile.

Jack winked at her.

'So are we on?' He returned his attention to Angela. 'I could be with you in a few minutes.'

'If you're sure?' She sounded reluctant. 'I wouldn't want to disrupt your work schedule.'

'I'm never too busy to come to the rescue of a lady in distress,' he replied before hanging up.

Locally Jack Brewer was known as Jack The Lad, a nickname he had reputedly earned from the number of hearts he was rumoured to have broken. Isobel listened to the exchange between him and her daughter with a sinking heart. She liked Jack but hoped Angela wasn't going to be his next conquest. Pleasant company though he was, in Isobel's opinion he was not good boyfriend material.

'Did you get all that?' he asked Isobel as he shrugged on his jacket.

'Yes,' she replied. 'Don't worry about me. You get on. Angela will be waiting for you.'

'Is there anything I can get you?' Jack asked, hunting round for his car keys.

'I'm fine,' Isobel replied. 'I've got my order book here so I'll go through that. I need to do some forward planning. There's a reception I hope to be able to cater at the end of next month and I need to start ordering in supplies. Off you go.'

* ★ ★

'Higher,' Mikey insisted as Angela pushed the garden swing.

'Hang on tight,' she laughed.

The ropes creaked from the pressure of Mikey's excited wriggling on the old wooden seat. The swing was strung from a tree and hadn't been used in a long time. Angela had seen Mikey swinging disconsolately to and fro while she had been waiting for Jack to come and collect her. Her offer to push had been met with enthusiastic acceptance.

'I used to play on this swing with your aunt when we were children,' Angela told Mikey, whose face was wreathed in a smile of pure pleasure. His happy laughter rung out as he kicked his heels and worked his legs backwards and for- wards to gain more height.

'Steady,' Angela cautioned him as the heel of his shoe nearly caught her in the face. 'We don't want any accidents.'

'You can catch me if I fall,' Mikey called back.

'I think you should stop now.' Angela tried to slow him down but Mikey was too hyped up to heed her warning.

'Just a bit longer, please,' he pleaded, throwing his head back and tugging at the ropes again.

A flash of colour caught the corner of Angela's eye as a car swept down the drive. It didn't look like Jack's, although Angela knew he did update them fairly frequently and he was always borrowing new models from the dealers to try out. All the same, Angela hardly thought a sedate family saloon was his style. The vehicle drew up outside the front doors and a woman clambered out of the back seat as the driver went round to the boot and began to unload suitcases.

'*Maman*, it's *Maman*,' Mikey squealed with delight and waved at the new arrival. The swing seat wobbled.

'Mikey, no,' Angela shrieked. Without warning the little boy leapt off the wooden seat as it began another upward swing.

She put out her arms to catch him

but she was too late. Mikey misjudged the drop and fell on the grass, groaned and rolled over, then lay perfectly still.

'No!' his mother screamed and ran towards the body lying on the grass, pushing Angela out of the way.

'Get away from my son,' she shouted.

She rolled Mikey over. His face was covered in wet earth and his clothes were stained green from the damp grass.

'*Chéri*,' Judith said, touching his cheek. 'Can you hear me?'

Mikey's eyelashes fluttered. He sighed then opened his eyes and beamed up at Angela.

'*Terrifique*,' he said in French. '*Encore une fois?*'

'This is all your fault.' Judith turned on Angela.

'No,' Angela protested.

'I saw everything.'

'It was an accident. Mikey, are you all right?'

'Don't touch him.' Judith's brown eyes flashed in anger. 'How dare you

55

put my son's life in danger.'

'I did no such thing,' Angela protested, still covered in guilt over what had happened.

'Where is his father?'

'In the studio.'

'He had no right leaving his son in the care of a servant.'

Angela bit down her retaliation. Judith was worried and annoyed and English was not her first language, but all the same Angela resented being referred to as a servant.

'Perhaps we should call a doctor,' she suggested in an effort to defuse the tension.

Mikey began to wriggle on the grass.

'I want to get up,' he complained, 'I'm cold and wet.'

'My poor angel.' Judith scooped him up in her arms and held the child to her chest. 'Your mother is here now. I will see no more harm comes to you.'

'Hello,' a voice broke into the scenario, 'what's going on here?'

'Jack,' Angela greeted him in relief. In

all the chaos no one had heard him arrive. 'Mikey fell off the swing.'

'Because you pushed him,' Judith insisted.

'Judith isn't it?' Jack smiled. 'You won't remember me but I was part of the set you used to hang around with when all we did was have beach parties and barbecues and go swimming and surfing. Those were the days.'

'Of course I remember you.' Judith released her hold on Mikey who seized the opportunity to scramble to his feet and run towards Angela.

'And this is Mikey is it? Hello young man.'

'Does it hurt anywhere?' Angela asked the child as he hid his face in her jumper.

'No.'

'Your head?'

'No but my new shirt is dirty.'

'Russ must drive us to the hospital. My son needs urgent medical attention. Where can he be?'

'I passed him on the way in,' Jack

said. 'He was looking for a puncture repair kit.'

'He should be here with his son.'

'Angela was keeping an eye on him,' Jack pointed out.

'And look what happened.'

'If you're really concerned about the little fellow, I can drive you to the surgery,' Jack offered.

'You have transport?'

He indicated his car.

'You don't mind do you?' Jack flicked no more than a casual glance in Angela's direction.

'I could come with you if you like?' she offered.

'You've done more than enough for one day,' Judith snapped. 'If you'd just help my son to the car, Jack?'

'I can walk,' Mikey protested.

'Best do as Mother says,' Jack replied, lifting the boy up in his arms. 'We don't want her upset do we, and you look as though you might be able to boast about a large bump on your head tomorrow morning.'

The child gazed at Jack with something like adoration on his face.

'Really?'

Judith turned the full power of her smile on Jack too and linked her arm through his.

'What about Russ?' Angela demanded.

'What about him?' Judith cast a casual glance over her shoulder.

'Surely someone should tell him what's happened?'

'You can do it if you like,' Judith replied. 'I need to get my son to the surgery. Now, Jack,' she turned back to him, 'are you sure there'll be room in your car for all of us?'

The trio made their way across the lawn to where Jack's sports car was parked next to Angela's abandoned bicycle. Behind her she heard the swing creak as it finally came to a stop.

5

The sky was ridged deep purple and scarred with vermilion streaks. Where it merged with the sea the horizon was shrouded in a faint scarlet mist. Angela wriggled her bare toes in the wet sand. It was damp and gritty and moved under the soles of her feet, just how she liked it. She had laced her trainers around her neck and stuffed her socks into the pocket of her jacket. Over the past eighteen months she had forgotten to look at sunsets. This one was pulling out all the stops.

The lengthening rays finally began to fade and a gentle breeze stirred the marram grass. Angela shivered as the temperature dropped. It had been a warm day for early spring but she could smell the beginnings of a light frost in the air.

'We should be getting back,' she said

to Russ, 'before the others begin to wonder where we are.'

They'd left Mikey in the care of his grandmother while they took time out to go for a stroll. Angela had put in extra hours that day polishing tables and work surfaces in preparation for a silent auction Pauline was holding at the weekend in aid of one of her charities, and Angela suspected Russ's suggestion of an early evening walk was prompted by Judith's seething anger over what had happened to their son.

Even though the incident had happened a few days ago there was no let-up in the atmosphere at Jacob's Bluff.

Doctor Hicks had examined Mikey and pronounced him fit but Judith was not prepared to let the matter drop. She had informed Angela that Mikey was no longer allowed to play on the swing and all further outings were to be supervised by a member of the family.

Angela couldn't shake off the feeling that Judith was spying on her as she went about her tasks. She'd hardly had a chance to be alone with Russ to apologise and every time she sat down for a break Judith would appear from nowhere and glare tellingly at her watch.

If it hadn't been for her mother, Angela would have handed in her notice, but she knew Isobel enjoyed her work and whilst Isobel Banks and Pauline Stretton were not exactly bosom friends, they were of an age where they were comfortable in each other's company.

'The little café behind the dunes should still be open. Do you fancy something warm to drink?' Russ suggested. 'If you're not in a hurry to get home? I haven't had much of a chance to talk to you since, well . . . ' He paused. 'I have been rather busy.'

'As have I,' Angela replied.

'Of course,' Russ agreed. 'Ma and I are very grateful for all you've done in Isobel's absence. How is she, by the way?' he asked.

'She had her cast removed the day

before yesterday.' Angela began rubbing her feet dry with the sleeve of her jumper.

'Tell her she's not to think of coming back to work until she's fully fit.'

'Your mother wants her back as soon as possible.'

'My mother's a tough old bird, she'll survive. Now about that drink?'

Angela took a deep breath.

'Plain speaking?' she demanded.

A look of alarm crossed Russ's face.

'I only had a hot chocolate in mind,' he insisted. 'I don't think I've got the energy for a challenging exchange of views.'

'If this is about Mikey then you can save yourself the cost of a hot chocolate. Judith has said everything that needs to be said on the subject. I've promised I won't go anywhere near the swing or take Mikey swimming or let him climb a tree or have a picnic on the beach or anything like that.' Angela's hazel eyes flashed. 'In a week or two I shall be out of your life so until then can we please drop the subject?'

The only sound between them was of the waves lapping the shore. Angela wished Russ wouldn't look at her so intently. The expression in his eyes was in danger of reducing her to a gauche fifteen-year-old, a mantle she thought she had long thrown off.

'Finished?' Russ enquired.

Angela nodded.

'Good, because I fancy some hot chocolate so the offer still stands, and I promise I'm not about to read you the riot act.'

Angela ran a hand through her tangled hair.

'I didn't mean to be rude but I've apologised so many times for what happened, I don't know what else to say. It was an accident and as far as I can tell Mikey suffered no lasting ill effects. Doctor Hicks confirmed that apart from one or two bruises there were no scars.'

'He's fine,' Russ re assured her, 'and it's what being a boy is all about isn't it?

Rough and tumble?'

'I'm not sure Judith sees it like that.'

'No bones were broken so for the third time of asking, do you want that hot chocolate?'

Angela hesitated.

'Does Stan still top it with toasted marshmallows?'

'There's only one way to find out, now come on before the tide comes in and washes us both away.'

Russ strode off in the direction of The Green Parrot.

'Russ, Angela,' the rotund proprietor greeted them after Russ propelled Angela through the doors of the steamy café. 'Good to see you. It's been too long. Sit down and make yourselves comfortable. Did you see the sunset? One of our best wouldn't you say? Quite brought out the romantic in me, so if you're not spoken for, Angela?' Stan twinkled at her.

'But you are, Stan Jones,' his wife called through from the back kitchen, 'don't you forget it.'

65

'What was that, my love?' Stan raised his eyes in mock exasperation.

'You heard.'

'Was there ever a man so henpecked?'

Smiling, Angela sat down opposite Russ. The dark circles under his eyes deepened in colour under the harsh café lighting. He stretched then stifled a yawn.

'I was working late last night on a rush job for some boardroom chairs for a prestigious client,' he explained.

'How are your chair-making skills these days?' Angela asked.

'Well I know my pine from my oak, and which glue to use — at least I hope I do.'

A complicit smile passed between them.

'This commission could lead to more orders so I want to make a good job of it. Trouble is they want them, like, yesterday. And you don't say no to these people if you want to stay on their good side.' He struggled with another yawn. 'I only managed to snatch a few hours' sleep and the bunk bed in the studio isn't very comfortable. My back hasn't been slow in letting me know all about it.'

Although Angela had not been inside Russ's studio she knew space was cramped.

'My son hates to have anything interfered with,' Pauline explained. 'Just leave some fresh sheets and towels out on the kitchen table and he'll pick them up when he's passing through.'

'You could try sleeping in a proper bed,' Angela suggested, 'there's plenty of room in the main house.'

Stan bustled over with two steaming mugs of chocolate.

'Enjoy,' he said.

Russ dunked hot marshmallows into the rich dark chocolate, frowning with concentration.

'You know that Judith and I are no longer married?'

'Your private life really is none of my business.' Angela hoped Russ wasn't about to be indiscreet.

'We have joint custody of Mikey.' Russ appeared not to have heard her interruption. 'And as my mother is better placed to look after him than Judith's mother he came back to England with me. Obviously Judith is missing him and that is why she can at times seem over-protective.'

'Why are you telling me all this?' Angela wriggled uncomfortably on her plastic seat, wishing now she'd passed on Russ's invitation.

'Because I have a feeling Judith suspects there is something going on between us.'

'That's ridiculous,' Angela protested.

'Ridiculous or not,' Russ conceded after a short pause, 'it's my feeling it's the reason she made such a fuss when Mikey fell off that wretched swing.'

Angela almost felt too embarrassed to ask the question, 'Why does she think we're in a relationship?'

'Mikey has been praising your skills a little too enthusiastically for comfort,'

Russ responded with a wry twist of his mouth.

'My skills?'

'The standard of your picnic fare; your football prowess; the number of scones you can eat at one sitting.' Russ listed them out. 'Living in the middle of Paris, Mikey's never been allowed to do any of those sorts of things before. There hasn't been the space and to my knowledge Judith has never baked a scone in her life.'

'If things are awkward would you like me to leave Jacob's Bluff before my mother comes back?'

'Certainly not,' Russ responded. 'I thought you ought to know how things stand that's all.'

'You make it sound like open warfare.'

'I would hate you to get hurt,' Russ smiled.

Angela's colour rose.

'I've faced up to a streetwise class of inner city adolescents, so a spat with Judith isn't going to rattle my cage.'

'I thought you'd say that.'

Angela took a long slurp of her chocolate.

'What's so funny?' She threw back her head in challenge, annoyed that Russ appeared to be taking her moral stand so lightly.

'You've got a large blob of chocolate froth on the end of your nose.' He produced a pristine white handkerchief. 'Do you want to use this to wipe it off?'

Refusing his offer, Angela ran the back of her hand across her face.

'Not the most ladylike of gestures,' he acknowledged, 'but it'll do.'

'Hey, shall I turn down the lighting?' Stan called over. 'My daughter has downloaded some lovely retro music, exactly the thing to go with hot chocolate.'

At the sound of the first number Angela's heartbeat trebled.

'Did you know this was going to happen?' she demanded.

A dimple dented Russ's cheek. 'I haven't bribed Stan, honest, but I can see by your face that you remember.'

It had been the night of Russ's eighteenth birthday party. His parents had pushed the boat out for their son's special day. Russ had looked unbelievably handsome. Although his birthday fell in the middle of December the French windows leading onto the terrace had been left open. Lanterns were strung from the awning, casting brilliant shadows on the flagstones. Strategically placed night torches illuminated the garden. The crisp air was alive with the sound of laughter, music and the popping of champagne corks.

It had been Angela's first grown-up party and Isobel had made her a new dress, a deep blue shift. Feeling immensely adult she and Cissie had watched the dancing, drinking lemonade from champagne flutes, pretending it was the real thing.

When Russ asked Angela to open the dancing with him, Cissie had given her a hefty shove in the back.

'His other girlfriends are looking

absolutely furious,' she hissed, 'so give it all you've got.'

Russ's hand circling her waist was firm as he guided her round the dance floor.

'Are you having a good time?' he asked.

Pleased she knew enough dance steps not to tread on his toes, she felt a smile of immense happiness light up her face.

'It's the most wonderful party I've ever been to,' she said, and she meant it.

A buffet table groaned with enough food to feed an army. Banners were strewn from the ceiling wishing Russ a happy eighteenth birthday, and at midnight a net of multi-coloured balloons suspended above them was due to be released onto the dance floor.

'I'm pleased to hear it,' he smiled, 'and thank you for the present.'

Angela had agonised for hours over what to give him. In the end she had settled for a special pen that could write upside down as well as the right way up and not run out of ink. In a spirit of extravagance she had had his initials engraved on the clip.

'I shall always treasure it,' Russ said as the music finished. 'Enjoy the rest of the evening.'

Cissie had teased Angela unmercifully afterwards.

'Stop it.' Angela had blushed a deeper shade of red. 'Russ was being kind, that's all.'

Eventually Cissie had tired of the game and dragged Angela across the room. 'Come on. I'm starving. Let's get to the food before it's all gone.'

'We've both changed a lot since then,' was Angela's careful reply to Russ's question.

'I can still remember what you were wearing,' Russ said. 'It was a blue dress.'

The dress was now wrapped in a lavender-scented travel bag and hung at the back of Angela's wardrobe. She had never worn it since but she absolutely refused to let Isobel re-work it into something more practical.

'I've still got the pen by the way and I use it every day.'

Angela scooped up her last marsh-mallow and popped it into her mouth. It was important to remember the past was another country.

'Russ, I'm no longer a plump teenager.' Russ opened his mouth to reply, but Angela stalled him. 'Judith?' she prompted.

'What about her?'

'She's still an issue.'

'Issue or not, Mikey is fretting because he's missing your company, so I thought it would be a nice idea if I took a day off from chair-making tomorrow and we all went down to the beach for a picnic.'

'All?'

'You, me and Mikey. It would give us a chance to re-bond.'

'I can hardly see Judith agreeing to that one.'

'Judith's going off somewhere with Jack Brewer.'

'Jack?'

'You don't mind do you?' Russ asked with a sharp look of enquiry.

'I'm surprised that's all.'

'He's offered to drive her around, show her some local scenery, revisit old haunts. So the beach?'

'I do have my other duties to see to.'

'I'm sure my mother won't mind if you take the day off.'

'Won't it look as though we're doing something behind Judith's back?'

'If there's any fallout I'll deal with it, but the forecast is good and we could all do with a bit of fresh air. Feel like playing hooky for the day?'

'Perhaps I do.'

It had to be the music getting to her, Angela decided. Why else would she have made such a decision?

'I'll pick you up at half past ten. Now how about another hot chocolate?'

6

'Angela,' Mikey yelled and waved from the window of the passenger seat of Russ's rickety new van, 'we're here.'

'Steady.' She heard Russ's admonishment to his son as they came to a halt on the patch of grass in front of Isobel's cottage.

Mikey scrambled out of his seat and grabbed his father's hand. Russ was wearing sweatshirt and jeans, while Mikey sported the cropped shorts and tee shirt that Angela had bought for him on a shopping trip Russ had arranged before Judith's arrival. Mikey's new wardrobe was probably something else Judith would hold against her, Angela thought with a sigh.

'We've got our swimming things.' Mikey swung his bag in the air, forcing Russ to take a quick sidestep.

'Put it back on the seat before

someone has an accident,' he begged.

Mikey tipped it through the open window.

'Did you remember the picnic?' He showed little sign of settling down.

'Manners, young man.' Russ placed a restraining hand on his shoulder. 'Say good morning to Mrs Banks.'

Isobel, who was now almost fully mobile, joined her daughter in the cottage doorway to greet the new arrivals. She smiled down at the excited child.

'You must be Mikey. How do you do?'

Mikey extended his hand in a formal gesture of greeting and mumbled a shy reply before asking, 'Are you Angela's mother?'

'I am,' she replied.

'My grandmother says you make lovely cakes and pies. Did you make any for us today?'

'Mikey, any more of that and the trip is cancelled,' Russ said in a firmer voice.

A look of horror crossed the little boy's face.

'You promised.' His lower lip began to wobble. 'You must never break a promise.'

'He's right, promises are made to be kept and he's only excited, that's all,' Isobel responded with a laugh. 'In answer to your question, Mikey, yes I have made an apple pie and a savoury one and I have also made as a treat a special cupcake for you with your name iced on it in blue letters.'

'You did?' Mikey's eyes were wide with delight. 'Where is it?'

'On the kitchen table.'

'Thank you,' he stammered, remembering his manners after his remarks earned him another look from his father.

'There's actually enough food in the cold bag to feed a small army,' Angela informed them, 'but you and I don't get cupcakes, Russ.'

'In that case the trip's definitely cancelled. Sorry,' he held up his hands, 'joke.' He tweaked Mikey's ear as the child looked about ready to burst into tears.

'Are you coming with us?' Mikey asked Isobel, quickly recovering from the drama.

'Good idea,' Russ added his voice to his son's invitation. 'It's a bit cramped in the van, but I'm sure we could all squash up.'

'Tempting though the offer is, I have to decline,' Isobel replied. 'My doctor would not be too pleased if I damaged my foot so soon after the plaster was removed. Besides I have a backlog of orders the length of which would make your eyes water and I've been asked to hold a class at the community centre. I must sort out a timetable.' Isobel beamed. 'Everyone's into baking these days.'

'Now my mother is back on her feet, she's raring to go.' Angela looked at her mother in mock exasperation.

'Where's the picnic?' Mikey was now hopping around from one foot to the other. 'Please,' he added after another quick glance at his father.

'Everything's in the kitchen,' Isobel replied, 'and you're quite right young man to get us back onto the important subject of food.'

'I'll get it,' Russ insisted as Isobel made to move towards the back of the cottage.

'You can carry my swimming things,' Angela informed Mikey, 'whilst I fetch the beach rug and umbrella.'

Five minutes later the van was packed and everyone was on board. Russ wound the window down to let in a breath of unseasonably warm air.

'All set?' he asked.

'Not sure what I'm sitting on.' Angela wriggled around. 'But it's digging in me.'

'As long as it isn't a tube of glue you're quite safe,' Russ replied.

'It's a book.' Angela produced a crumpled manual.

'I wondered where that went. In my spare time, of which I don't have much,

I've been reading up about tropical woods. Some are poisonous you know and it's best to know which ones to avoid. Put it on the dashboard. Now is everybody ready?'

Russ started the engine.

'Where are we going?' Angela asked as they trundled along the coast road.

'How about our bay?'

Angela knew exactly where Russ meant. She and Cissie had swum there during the endless summer holidays of their youth. There had been no need for adult supervision as it was tucked away in a small cove that only a few locals knew about. Together the two girls would spend lazy days, swimming, exploring and sun bathing, glad to escape the confines of school and all the other restrictions of their lives. The surfing set frequented the more commercial resorts further down the coast and the bay had remained an undiscovered gem. They had christened it 'our bay' and the name was used as a code word for secret meetings and secluded afternoons away from the rest of the world.

'Are you sure you wouldn't like to refresh your surfing skills?' Angela asked, fearing Russ might find the bay a bit too quiet.

'I was never that good,' Russ admitted, 'besides the sea's too calm to surf today. I think I'm in the mood to be lazy. How about you?'

'That suits me too,' Angela responded.

'I've brought my fishing net,' Mikey piped up from the rear of the van. 'Can we go looking for crabs in the rock pools?'

Russ glanced at his son's reflection in the mirror. 'As long as you stay in sight you can go wherever you like.'

'Are you sure Judith doesn't mind about this outing?' Angela voiced the suspicion niggling the back of her mind.

'She doesn't know,' Russ replied after a short pause.

'You didn't you tell her?' Angela's unease deepened.

'There was no reason to. She has

gone out for the day with Jack. I didn't ask her what they were going to do.'

Angela frowned. Was she being used as a pawn in some sort of sophisticated marriage game? Were Russ and Judith intent on making each other jealous, Judith with Jack and Russ by taking Angela out on a picnic with their son?

'Don't worry,' Russ reassured her, 'we'll be home long before she gets back from Norwich.'

'You said you didn't know where she'd gone,' Angela replied.

'I don't exactly but I overheard part of her telephone conversation with Jack before she left this morning and I thought Norwich was mentioned.'

Russ concentrated on negotiating a tricky turn. The van swayed slightly before righting itself.

'Still getting the hang of things.' Russ tapped the steering wheel. 'She can be a bit temperamental. Jack got her for me. What do you think of my new wheels?'

'They've certainly seen a bit of life.'

'The van was well within my budget,' Russ admitted, 'and I didn't want anything too smart. I'm always scraping gateposts and some of the places I visit are pretty hazardous.'

'Are we nearly there yet?' Mikey demanded.

'Five minutes,' Russ promised.

While father and son embarked on a spirited game of I-spy, Angela tried to quell her anxiety about this outing. Was she worrying unnecessarily? If there was nothing to worry about why hadn't Russ told Judith of their plans? There was nothing to hide. Maybe that was why he hadn't told her, she reasoned. It was perplexing being able to see both sides of the argument and it had kept Angela tossing and turning into the small hours.

She decided she would be pleased when her mother returned to Jacob's Bluff. With the approaching summer term, Angela needed to register with an agency to see what teaching posts were available and she couldn't do that until she had finished her stint at the house.

'It's your mother's birthday on Easter Sunday, isn't it?' Russ asked.

'Fancy you remembering.' Angela turned to him in surprise. 'And yes, this year it falls on Easter Sunday.'

'I would like to give her something special to show my appreciation for all the work she's done for the family.'

'What do you have in mind?' Angela asked.

'A book case or a set of shelves? What do you think?'

'The sitting room floor is littered with reference books,' Angela agreed. 'There are piles of them all over the place and I am worried she might trip up and do more damage to her foot.'

'Good idea.'

'Could you do it?' Angela asked.

'Bookcases I can do in my sleep.' Russ flashed her a smile. 'I'll get cracking on it as soon as I can.'

'You must let me make a contribution.'

'Wouldn't hear of it. I'll get Ma to chip in. She'd like to show her appreciation too.'

'In that case thank you. It will be a lovely surprise.'

'By the way, a bit more news,' Russ said. 'A big horse-racing stud has asked me to tender for a dining-room suite. Until now they've been entertaining in local restaurants, but it's costly and it takes a huge chunk out of the day, driving there and back and all the rest of it. So, they are converting some old stables into a state-of-the-art catering suite and they want me to provide the furniture.'

'That's wonderful,' Angela enthused, 'but surely you won't have time for a bookcase?'

'I like to keep occupied of an evening and something simple like a bookcase helps me de-stress. You've no idea how demanding some of these corporate customers can be. My trouble is I don't like turning down work.'

'You sound exactly like my mother.'

'I can see the sea,' Mikey piped up. 'Look.' He pointed an excited finger towards the stretch of blue water sparkling in the sunshine.

'I suggest we park behind the dunes,' Russ said. 'We don't want to get stuck in the sand. If my memory serves me correctly there's a bit of hard standing and it won't be too far to stagger with all our kit. Why we had to bring so much is beyond me. Anyone would think we were going to stay for a fortnight.'

Feeling as excited as Russ's son, Angela jumped out of the van, followed by an eager Mikey who scrambled over the back seat.

'You're going to teach me how to play beach cricket aren't you, Papa? I'm having first go with the bat.'

He grabbed it up out of the kit bag and made to run off in the direction of the dunes.

'Hey, young man,' Russ called after him, 'not so fast, come back. That's better. Now, you take this.' He loaded

Mikey up with a small mountain of beach bits and pieces. 'Right, off you go.'

'He'll fall or drop something.' Angela watched the child's progress with an anxious look.

'Do him good,' Russ grinned. 'Don't worry. He's got loads of energy and I want him to work some of it off before I demonstrate my lack of prowess with the beach bat, otherwise he'll beat me hands down. My skills are more than rusty.'

'Mine are nonexistent,' Angela laughed.

'In that case you can man the wicket.'

'Isn't that a rather dangerous position?'

'Not as long as you remember to duck.'

Angela let Mikey and Russ go for a dip while she sorted out the rug and beach umbrella. The sun was strong but there was a chill breeze coming off the water. Picking a sheltered spot, she settled down with a magazine. In the background she could hear the two males splashing around in the water, Mikey shrieking as his father lifted him high in the air, then pretended to drop him back in the water.

'Come on in,' Russ called out to Angela.

The idea of wriggling into her swimsuit behind a rock did not appeal to her.

'I've only got time for a paddle,' she said by way of excuse.

'Go and fetch her, Mikey,' Russ nudged his son towards Angela, 'and don't take no for an answer.'

Laughing, the child tugged her towards the water.

'It's so cold your toes will drop off, won't they, Papa?'

'We couldn't let that happen.' Russ put out a hand and clasping Angela's drew her into his arms. 'There, that's better isn't it?'

'You're wet.'

She did her best to wriggle away from him but Russ had firm hold of her wrist. His lips grazed hers. They tasted of sand and salt water. She could feel prickles of stubble grazing the side of her face as she turned away in protest.

'Had enough?'

'Think so,' Angela stuttered, not sure if she was cold or on fire and whether Russ was referring to the cold or his kiss. Her senses were all over the place.

'I'm cold.' Mikey shivered and began to run back up the beach.

Finally freeing herself of Russ's hand, Angela hurried after the child and produced a huge fluffy towel and wrapping him in it, rubbed him dry.

'Want me to dry your feet?' Russ asked Angela as he strolled up behind his son.

His pale skin glistened with water. Angela passed him a second towel then looked away.

'I can do them myself, thank you,' she said firmly.

'Come on then, Mikey, let's go and change while Angela tends to her feet.'

By the time they returned Angela had recovered her equilibrium and her feet were dry. She was perched primly on the rug, going through the contents of the picnic basket.

'I presume you're both hungry?'

'After all that activity I'm starved,' Russ replied. 'Mikey?'

'Me too,' he squealed.

The keen air appeared to have whipped everyone's appetite into shape and Isobel's picnic was demolished with unseemly haste. The cupcake was duly admired before it too suffered the same fate as the savoury pie.

'Right.' Russ unzipped the holdall after he'd indulged in a quick snooze in the sunshine. 'After that feast, we now need to run round to work some of it off.'

Angela groaned. 'I couldn't move.'

'You're going to have to.' Russ nudged her awake with his foot. 'Remember you're wicket-keeper. Come on, Mikey. You hold the bat like this.'

Grumbling, Angela crouched behind Mikey who side-swiped the ball Russ bowled at him. He made an impatient gesture in French as the makeshift wicket went flying.

'Careful, you nearly got Angela's legs,' Russ called out as she tossed the ball back to him.

'I do not understand why I cannot hit the ball,' Mikey whimpered.

'Try another one,' Angela coaxed after she'd rebuilt the wicket.

Mikey's second attempt to hit the ball fared no better than his first. He stamped his foot in the sand. 'This is no fun any more.' He threw down the bat and watched it bounce back into the air.

'Mikey,' Russ warned his son in a sharp voice, 'less of that.'

'*Maman*.' Mikey's pout disappeared in an instant. Angela spun round, dropping the ball in dismay.

'So this is where you all are.'

Judith stood silhouetted against the backdrop of the dunes. She was wearing a stunning one-piece black bathing costume under a colourful beach robe.

She walked towards them with the assurance of a trained model. Her skin was beautifully tanned and although the brisk wind was now whipping the crested waves to an alarming height, Judith looked confident and relaxed.

'*Chéri.*' She kissed Russ on the cheek. 'You should have told me you were planning a day out on the beach — with a picnic too I see.' She glanced down at the remains of their lunch. 'You have been eating a veritable feast. All I had was one nasty cup of coffee.' She shivered. 'The English have no idea how to make a proper coffee.'

'Where's Jack?' Russ asked.

'There was an emergency at the garage so we had to cut short our day. Pauline told me where you were and I decided to join you. Jack dropped me off but unfortunately he could not stay.'

Judith trailed a finger down Russ's cheek in a playfully provocative gesture.

'Now what is this game you are playing? May I join in?'

Ignoring Angela, Judith picked up

her discarded ball.

'I throw it like this, no? Come on, my darling,' she spoke in French to her son, 'hit it for me.'

With a happy laugh Mikey now connected with the ball and sent it soaring into the air.

'Quick, Russ!' Judith shaded her eyes against the sun. 'It's going to fall into the sea. Catch it.'

With much splashing and laughing, both Mikey and Russ raced into the sea to obey her command. Turning away from the happy family scene, Angela began to repack the picnic basket.

'When you've finished clearing up,' Judith ambled over to Angela, 'perhaps you'd take the things back to Russ's van and wait for us there until we're ready to leave?'

With no more than a cursory glance in Angela's direction, Judith dropped the discarded bat at her feet; then, laughing, ran into the water to join Russ.

'Now, Mikey,' she said to her son, 'we

need to teach you how to swim properly. It's important for you not to be scared of water. Brr, it's cold.'

The sun disappeared behind a cloud, casting a shadow on the beach. Not bothering to look up, Angela crammed everything back into the basket and began to lug it up the sand dunes to where Russ had parked the van.

7

'As it's your last day perhaps you'd clean my room.' Judith's smile didn't reach her eyes. 'It hasn't been done since I arrived and it is in rather a mess.'

Angela would have liked to refuse but there was no point in making a fuss, she decided as she picked up her cleaning box and headed towards the stairs. From tomorrow her mother would be back at Jacob's Bluff and Isobel and Pauline Stretton could work out the cleaning schedule between them.

Angela pushed open the door to Judith's bedroom and gasped. Articles of clothing were strewn over the mirror and across the back of chairs. The dressing table was a mess of spilt face powder and make-up and the top had been left off a jar of face cream. The contents had oozed down the side leaving a sticky trail. Judith's black swimsuit dangled from the wardrobe door handle and her damp bathing towel had been draped over the radiator.

Angela flung open the bedroom window to get rid of the cloying smell of the heavy perfume Judith favoured. She looked back at the room in despair. It was difficult to know where to start. Pulling back the covers to air the bed, she gathered up Judith's laundry and thrust it into the wicker basket in the corner of the room.

An ornate mahogany jewellery box was also open on the bedside table. Angela closed the lid with a firm click.

Mikey's laughter floated up from the garden and glancing out of the window, Angela saw Pauline Stretton on the lawn doing her best to cope with a bat as her grandson bowled balls towards her.

'No, Grandma.' He skipped across the lawn. 'Like this.'

Angela watched Mikey demonstrate

the correct technique of hitting the ball.

'See? It's easy. Now, you try,' he insisted.

A smile softened Angela's lips as Pauline gritted her teeth and waited for Mikey to bowl.

'Bravo.' He clapped his hands as Pauline's bat met its target and she lobbed the tennis ball high into the air.

They both watched it soaring upwards, then as it began to descend Mikey did his best to catch it.

'Never mind,' Pauline commiserated with him as it fell through his fingers, 'I did give it quite a wallop.'

'What's a wallop?' Mikey asked.

'A big hit.'

'Wallop, wallop,' Mikey chanted as he did a few practice throws of the ball.

'Where did you learn to play this game?' Pauline asked.

'Angela showed me yesterday on the beach. We were playing before *Maman* arrived. Then we went swimming with Papa. Only Angela didn't come with us. She carried all the things back to the van. After that we came home.'

Angela turned away from the window. That about summed up her afternoon. Judith's unscheduled arrival had taken all the fun out of the day and after Angela had loaded the picnic and the umbrella and rugs into the back of Russ's van, she'd sat in the passenger seat alone and waited for the family to finish their swim.

It was half an hour before they straggled back. Judith's arm was linked through Russ's and Mikey ran along in front of them. Angela watched Russ bend his head forward and laugh at something Judith whispered in his ear, and did her best to ignore the slow burning anger in the pit of her stomach. How dare Russ use her in this way? She supposed she only had herself to blame. She should have realised what was going on. Russ wanted to win back his wife and Angela was a convenient fall guy. As a ruse, it had succeeded one hundred per cent. Judith was very much back in the family fold and

Angela was left to clear up his ex-wife's messy bedroom.

The en-suite shower was as bad as the bedroom and giving vent to her annoyance on the smeared glass cubicle, Angela was breathing heavily by the time she finished. Her shirt clung to her back. She would have liked to indulge in a shower herself, but there wasn't time. Cleaning Judith's room meant she had fallen behind with her other chores and she didn't want Pauline breathing down her back demanding to know why she hadn't started on the downstairs rooms.

Angela yanked Judith's sheets back onto the bed. With a loud thud her handbag fell onto the floor, spilling the contents over the carpet. Stifling her irritation Angela knelt down to pick it up. Something hard dug into her knee. Pulling aside the bed cover, she discovered Judith's wallet stuffed full of bank notes. Was this another of Judith's tricks? It would be the easiest thing in the world to blame Angela for its loss.

She had been the only other person in the bedroom and if Judith's wallet went missing, suspicion would naturally fall on Angela. Branding her a thief would nicely finish the hatchet job on her integrity.

Ramming the wallet back into the bag, Angela snapped the clasp shut then put it on the bedside cabinet. She finished making the bed, then picking up Judith's handbag she made her way downstairs and out into the garden to where Pauline and Mikey were now enjoying early elevenses.

'Angela,' Mikey greeted her, 'will you play beach cricket with me? Grandma says she is too tired.'

'It's my hip, I'm afraid.' Pauline gave an embarrassed smile. 'Think I've overdone it. Would you like some lemonade, Angela? Homemade? Help yourself. There's plenty.'

'Thank you.' Angela poured out a glass.

'Sit down. There's no need to stand on ceremony. Are you all right?' Pauline asked. 'Your cheeks are very red.'

'I found this in Judith's bedroom.' Angela produced her bag, hoping her hand wasn't shaking too much.

'What were you doing in Judith's room?' Pauline asked with a frown.

'Cleaning it.'

'You didn't have to do that.'

'She asked me to.'

'Did she indeed?'

Pauline looked at the wallet Angela was now clutching, having extracted it from Judith's bag.

'The thing is,' she did her best to keep her voice steady, 'there's a lot of money in her wallet and I wouldn't want it going astray. I found it under the bed, hidden in the covers.'

'Perhaps you had better give it to me.' Pauline held out her hand.

Angela passed the bag over and watched her place it carefully under one of the cushions.

'It will be perfectly safe with me.'

'Thank you.'

'Now tell me, have you enjoyed your

time here?' Pauline lapsed into a smile. 'I can see by the expression on your face you're in the mood to give me an honest answer.'

'Would you expect anything less?' Angela asked.

'If it's any consolation I have found your presence here most helpful and I'd have been lost without you. I know we've had our moments but,' Pauline's face softened, 'it's nice to have a bit of life about the place. I hate it when all the ladies on my committee agree with me. I like a confrontation I can get my teeth into.'

'We have had one or two of those,' Angela admitted as Pauline smoothed down Mikey's hair in a grandmotherly gesture. The little boy clung onto her knee and hummed a happy tune.

'It was quite like the old days,' Pauline confided, 'when you challenged my decisions.' She held up a hand. 'I'm not about to re-visit any of them and in retrospect I have reluctantly to admit on occasions you were right. I don't always move with the times.' Pauline paused. 'Why don't you go and play on your bike for a while, Mikey?' she suggested. 'You can cycle down to the studio but no further.'

'Brilliant. Bye, Angela.'

He scampered away.

'Now shall I say it for you?' Pauline poured out some more lemonade. 'It's Judith isn't it?'

'I can't help feeling the wallet full of money was a test.'

'To see if you were honest?'

'Her jewellery box was open too. There were rings and bracelets in it.'

'Then that was very wrong of her.' Pauline put the jug back on the table. 'To put your mind at rest, I wouldn't for one moment have suspected you of dishonesty and Judith would have had a battle on her hands if she'd come to me with tales of pilfering. So, no more needs to be said on the subject.'

'Thank you,' Angela said in a quiet voice.

'I sent Mikey down to the studio because I wouldn't want him to hear what I have to say about his mother. I don't normally talk about people behind their backs but this time I feel it is necessary.' Pauline took a deep breath. 'Judith has always been a disruptive influence. It's in her nature. She is a female who needs to be the centre of attention. When she isn't she does things, if you can understand my meaning. This time you were the target of her emotions.'

'Why did she choose me?'

'There's no doubt Judith loves her son and even though she and Russ are no longer together, she doesn't want another woman stepping into her shoes.'

'Russ and I are good friends, nothing more.'

Angela was still inwardly seething at the way Russ had treated her and refused to acknowledge how she had been attracted to his physique when he had been swimming on the beach.

'I was always his younger sister's best friend.'

'You've grown up a bit since you were a plump little girl with pigtails. Anyway what are you going to do now that your time here is over? Have you any plans? If you want a reference for a new teaching post I'd be pleased to provide one.'

'I've been commissioned to do a thesis on the environment by the board of the local school.' Angela shook off her worries as she went on to explain, 'Then if they like what I have to say, I may be offered the post of running the junior wing. The advert said they were looking for a committed individual with enterprise, keen on social issues, with progressive ideas that incorporate family values.'

'And you think you can do it?'

'It's a marvellous opportunity,' Angela enthused.

'I had heard of the vacancy.'

'You didn't influence things did you?'

'I have too much respect for your

106

professionalism to do that,' Pauline replied. 'I know you can manage perfectly well without my input, but I think you are ideal for the post and if asked for my opinion as an impartial outsider then that is what I would say.'

Angela blinked not knowing quite how to respond.

'I've never known you lost for words before,' Pauline teased. 'You're going to have to come up with something better than a confused silence if you want to convince the governors that you are the person for the job.'

'I feel as though I may have misjudged you in the past.'

'Don't start apologising for heaven's sake.' Pauline put up a hand to stop her. 'I couldn't cope with it. I suggest our relationship goes on much as before. I hate it when people are sickeningly nice to me. I thought you were different. You're not going to change are you?'

'You know me better than that, Mrs Stretton,' Angela replied.

'Good. My husband and I used to have very stimulating exchanges and it's something I sorely miss. By the way,' she added, 'in an effort to modernise my relationship with your mother I've asked her to start calling me Pauline. It's what you young people do these days isn't it? Call everyone by their first name?'

'Is that an invitation for me to do the same?' Angela queried, not sure if she had understood the implication.

Pauline Stretton would deem that being invited to use her first name would be a great honour and not something to be offered lightly but Angela was anxious not to misread the situation.

'It wouldn't be forsaking any of your principles would it?' Pauline asked with a twinkle in her eye.

'It wouldn't, so thank you, Pauline,' Angela added.

'Good, that's settled then.'

A shadow fell across the lawn between them.

'Judith,' Pauline greeted the new-comer, 'where have you been?'

'I was restless so I went for a walk.'

'Then you've hardly worn the right shoes. The grass is very wet. You should have taken a pair of boots from the cold room.'

'I passed Mikey — ' Judith ignored her remark. ' — on his bike. He said you gave permission for him to cycle down to the studio.' She glared at Angela.

'I told him he could go,' Pauline replied. 'It's good exercise for the child. Now I have something to important to discuss with you.'

'Yes?' Judith sounded disinterested. 'Where's Russ?' she asked.

'I have no idea.' Pauline delved underneath the cushion of her recliner. 'Here is your bag.'

'Where did you find it?' Judith asked.

'I didn't. Angela did. She also found your wallet full of money.' Pauline passed it over. 'I would suggest in future you take better care of your valuables.'

The look that crossed Judith's face convinced Angela her suspicions had been well founded.

'Also, from tomorrow Isobel Banks will be back. Her duties will not include cleaning your room. If you are looking for something to do whilst you are staying in my house, I suggest that you take on responsibility for your own and Mikey's rooms. You seem to have plenty of time on your hands.'

'I do not clean rooms.'

'Then you'll forgive me for saying I hope you make your stay here as short as possible.'

'I, er . . . ' Angela stood up. ' . . . think I'll get on. Thank you for the lemonade, Pauline.'

'I'll take the tray back to the kitchen,' Judith offered, snatching it off the table. 'It's Pauline now is it?' she hissed in Angela's ear as they walked across the lawn.

Against her better judgement, Angela began to feel sorry for Judith.

'I know you're worried about being

separated from your son and that you see me as some sort of threat to your position as his mother,' she said, 'but you have no need to worry. Russ and I are good friends and the thought of our relationship being anything else is quite frankly a bit of a laugh.'

Angela relieved Judith of the tray and carried it into the kitchen to find Russ seated at the table. From the expression on his face it was obvious he had heard every word. Angela hid a small smile of satisfaction as she put the tray down on the draining board and began to wash the glasses under the tap.

As a parting shot she couldn't have done better. Whatever was going on here between Russ and Judith, she was pleased to be out of it.

8

The garden was full to overflowing as groups of people stood around, chatting, catching up on local gossip and sipping their drinks.

Angela was doing the rounds offering trays of canapés to the guests. Ever since the plans for the Easter party had been finalised she had been anxious to take the strain off her mother, who had insisted on overseeing all the arrangements.

'We don't want your foot going back to square one. Remember what the doctor said.' Angela confronted Isobel in the kitchen on the day of the party.

'Darling,' Isobel looked up from stirring a fragrant sauce that was making Angela's mouth water, 'don't fuss. I am absolutely fine. Now where are those prawns?'

'It's your birthday, we should all be

waiting on you.'

'It also happens to be Easter Sunday and I have an Easter egg hunt to arrange.' Isobel cast an anxious glance out of the window. 'I do hope none of the children find them too early. I did my best to hide them but youngsters are so clever these days.' Isobel sighed. 'Thank heavens no one has brought along a dog. They can sniff out chocolate like nobody's business.'

'Now who's fussing?' Angela put an arm around her mother's shoulders.

'It's a hostess's prerogative.' Isobel hugged her back. 'Do you think I've done enough salmon?'

Angela scooped up a platter of cocktail sausages.

'There's enough of everything, now come on. You're neglecting your guests and in case you hadn't noticed they are in the garden.'

The lunchtime sunshine was pleasantly warm, causing Isobel to hastily rearrange her plans.

'It's so much easier to have everyone outside. If there any spillages we won't spend ages getting stains out of the carpets, or vacuuming up crumbs for hours after everyone has gone.'

Angela had to agree with her mother on that one. Isobel had insisted on inviting all their friends and neighbours to thank them for their help during her period of incapacitation and as her birthday happened to fall on Easter Sunday, it seemed a good idea to combine it with an Easter egg hunt for the children.

'Did you have to invite everybody?' Angela complained as they received yet more acceptances.

'I didn't think they would all come,' Isobel admitted.

'Of course they're going to come. They know a good thing when they see it. Your cooking is renowned throughout the district.'

'Need any help?' Jack Brewer poked his head through the back door of the kitchen.

'Just the person,' Isobel greeted him with a beaming smile. 'Could you top up the drinks? There's a makeshift bar by the shed.'

'I'm your man. Here, let me.'

He relieved Isobel of the tray of glasses she had picked up.

'Thanks, Jack,' Angela greeted him with a kiss on the cheek. 'I've been trying to persuade Mum to take things easy but I'm not getting anywhere.'

'Why don't you go and open that huge pile of presents on the garden table,' Jack suggested, 'and leave Angela and me to run the show?'

Isobel hesitated and Angela pushed home Jack's advantage. 'It would be rude not to thank people personally.'

'My foot is aching a bit,' Isobel admitted.

'Go on then, shoo. Out you go.' Jack nudged Isobel into the garden. 'Make way for the birthday girl,' he bellowed, 'and will someone please ensure she sits down to open her presents?'

A round of applause broke out as

Isobel made her smiling way through a sea of guests.

'Thanks, Jack,' Angela murmured in his ear. 'Mum can be a bit of a handful at times.'

'My pleasure.' He hefted his tray of glasses aloft. 'Catch up later?'

The next hour passed in a whirl and Angela's feet now also began to ache as she circulated with yet more trays of party food. She knew from past experience that no one would want to leave early, especially not until the Easter egg hunt was over. Then there was afternoon tea to be served. She and her mother had iced a two-tier birthday cake and decorated it with Easter bonnets and tiny marzipan chicks and it now held pride of place on the buffet table.

With much giggling more mothers herded young children through the side gate of the cottage.

'We're not too early are we?' one anxious parent asked. 'Young Harry was so excited about the Easter egg hunt, he couldn't wait.'

'Everybody is welcome.' Angela hoped her smile didn't give away her mounting anxiety. She hadn't realised quite how many people her mother had invited.

'What on earth is making that dreadful noise?' Jack demanded as a delivery van drew up on the greensward outside in a belch of exhaust fumes.

'I've no idea,' Angela answered, 'but I do hope my mother hasn't invited a courier company to join us.'

'Nothing would surprise me,' Jack murmured.

'Me neither,' Angela agreed.

The driver jumped out and opening the doors disappeared inside the van.

'Special delivery,' he announced, 'for Mrs Isobel Banks.'

'Russ?' Angela squinted into the sunshine. 'Is that you?'

'Come to deliver one bookcase for the birthday girl. It was too big to get into my van so I hired this one. Sorry about the exhaust.' He coughed. 'Think it needs seeing to. Jack, just the man,'

Russ greeted him. 'Lend a hand.'

'I'm not mending your exhaust,' he protested.

'Help me with the bookcase.'

Jack scratched his head. 'We won't be able to get round the back. There are too many people.'

'Hang on.' Angela, who had followed Jack, turned back to the cottage; and pushing open the front door, moved a couple of tables out of the way. 'This way. Are you sure you can manage?'

'No problem. Whoops. Language,' Russ chided Jack as a loud bump was followed by a robust curse.

'It's all right for you,' Jack grumbled. 'You've got the easy end. Cover your ears, Angela. There might be a few more where that came from. This thing is heavy.'

After a few false starts the two men eventually manoeuvred the bookcase into the sitting room.

'Whew.' Jack wiped his brow as they steadied it upright. 'If I'd known what I was in for, I'd have sat on my hands and let you get on with it on your own, Stretton.'

Angela ran her fingers over the newly polished wood and inhaled the smell of pine.

'Thank you, Russ, it's wonderful. You've been far too generous.'

'Ma made a contribution too. Well, she didn't sand it down,' Russ laughed, 'but she paid up. Glad you like it. Do you think Isobel will approve?'

'She'll love it.'

'Hate to point out the obvious,' Jack said, looking round with a puzzled frown, 'but you seem to have forgotten the shelves.'

'I'll go and get them.'

'Glad he didn't wrap it up.' Jack stepped back to admire the piece of furniture. 'He'd have run out of paper.'

'It's his family's birthday gift to my mother,' Angela explained.

'Shall I fetch her from the garden?' Jack asked.

'Let's set it up first.'

'Here we are.' Russ was back with the

shelves. 'Want me to fit them now?'

'Please,' Angela replied.

'You'd best give me one of Isobel's books to help gauge the height,' Russ said, sizing up the side struts.

He cast Angela an enquiring look.

'Anything wrong?'

'No.'

Angela hurriedly picked up a discarded book off the floor. This was her first meeting with Russ since she had stopped working at Jacob's Bluff and she had no idea what to say to him or how things stood between them. She could still remember the look in his eyes after she'd scoffed at Judith's allegations about their relationship and how she'd insisted the French girl's suspicions were ridiculous. Angela's feeling of satisfaction had soon evaporated and she had been left feeling rather flat as Russ had finished his coffee and gone back to his studio.

Isobel, who was now working back at the house, confirmed that Judith hadn't returned to France and as far as she knew had no immediate intention to do so.

Angela knew from the temporary teaching post she had acquired that Mikey had been enrolled for the summer term at St Andrew's and was due to start after Easter.

'Don't get them crooked,' Jack instructed Russ as he inserted a small bracket into the slot.

'Here.' Russ passed over one of the shelves. 'If you've got such a good eye, you can have a go. You have to count the number of slots and make sure they match up to get it even.'

'Jack's only trying to help,' Angela intervened and received a monosyllabic grunt in reply.

'Judith not with you, Russ?' Jack asked casually as he inserted a shelf into its correct slot.

Angela recalled Jack's date with Judith on the day of the picnic and wondered if that was why Russ was so snappy.

'She and my mother are on their way.

They thought a whole day's party might be too much for Mikey, so they're bringing him along for the Easter egg hunt later.'

'You have to stay on too,' Angela insisted.

'I'm not really dressed for a party.' Russ was covered in more than his usual number of wood shavings.

'Dress code is casual,' Angela insisted.

Jack eyed Russ's work apron. 'It depends how you interpret the word casual.' His eyes were alight with mischief as he added, 'But I'm sure Isobel won't mind.'

'What won't I mind?' a voice interrupted from the doorway.

'Russ has delivered your birthday present, Mum, it's from him and Pauline,' Angela explained.

'Don't forget Mikey, he put in some pocket money too,' Russ added.

'Jack and I are trying to persuade Russ to stay on but he says he's not dressed for a party.'

'What nonsense. Of course you've

got to stay on,' Isobel insisted, 'you'll need some sustenance after all your hard work, Russ.' She advanced into the room. 'What a wonderful present,' she said, kissing Russ's cheek. 'I love it to bits. At last I'll have somewhere proper to put all my books. You shouldn't have been so generous.'

'Glad you like it, Isobel.' Russ produced a scarlet bow trimmed in gold attached to a business card, and placed it on the middle shelf. 'Perhaps you'd put the word round if people ask who made it?'

'Nothing like touting for publicity.' Jack raised his eyebrows.

'Of course I will tell people all about you. I'll praise your work to the skies. Marketing is something I understand.' Isobel cast a reproving glance at Jack. 'Now I insist you relax. Angela, take Russ into the garden and look after him, there's a good girl.'

'You're not going to attack that mountain of washing-up in the kitchen are you?' Angela asked. 'You've an army of fit young men in the garden. They can do it.'

'I don't think one can ask guests to help out.'

'Tell them there aren't enough plates to go round for dessert,' Jack added his voice to the cause. 'That'll galvanise them into action.'

'In that case, Jack,' Isobel suggested with a sweet smile, 'as you've sorted out the washing-up rota so efficiently, you could pass me my books off the floor whilst I place them on the shelves.'

'I knew it was a mistake standing around with my hands in my pockets,' Jack grumbled. 'You go and enjoy yourself, Angela, while I stay indoors on this lovely afternoon and do all the work.'

'Stop being so grumpy and pass me a book,' Isobel laughed.

'Ma mentioned something about a commissioned thesis?' Russ said as he and Angela made their way into the garden.

'I've been working on it,' Angela

replied, relieved he wasn't going to refer to the incident in the kitchen at Jacob's Bluff. 'I've got until May to submit it.'

Russ accepted a loaded plate of food from young Harry's mother, who was helping out with the buffet.

'It's for the two of you,' Mrs Wilkes explained. 'Angela hasn't eaten anything yet. The poor girl has been rushed off her feet. There's a spare seat over there.' She pointed to a wooden bench. 'Why don't you and Russ take cover under the trees, Angela? The Easter egg hunt is about to start and you don't want to get flattened in the rush. Look at my Harry. Talk about eager.'

The little boy was already organising the younger visitors into teams.

It was relatively secluded under the trees and Angela settled down beside Russ while they set about the business of satisfying their hunger.

'Didn't mean to scoff.' Russ finished his last bit of savoury pie with a shamefaced smile. 'I forgot to get any breakfast this morning and I was up early to finish off your mother's present.'

'Do you want any dessert?' Angela scooped up the last of her cold curry. 'If I can find any clean plates?'

'Later perhaps.' Russ leaned against the back of the wooden bench. 'I've missed you,' he said quietly, 'and I know I owe you an apology.'

'You don't owe me anything, Russ,' she insisted.

'Ma told me what happened with Judith and the jewellery box.'

'Your mother dealt with the situation very well.'

'I don't want Mikey to be torn between two warring parents, and Judith knows this. She also knows I won't go against her and she plays on it. I'm sorry you got caught up in it all.'

'It doesn't matter now,' Angela replied. 'In future I shouldn't cross paths that often with Judith.'

'Don't speak too soon.' Russ nodded towards yet more new arrivals.

'Angela.' Mikey sped towards them,

arms outstretched. 'I've found an egg. Look.'

'Not sure if you're supposed to have started looking for them yet,' Russ chided his son.

'It was under that tree.'

Mikey pointed to where Jack and Judith were engaged in animated conversation. A warm flush worked its way up Angela's neck. Was Judith still playing games? Glad she was out of the complicated love triangle, Angela smiled at the little boy.

'Why don't you go and share the egg with some of the other boys? They'll be your new classmates when term starts next week.'

'OK.' Still clasping his foil-wrapped egg, Mikey joined a group of children busy searching the flowerbeds for more eggs. 'I've got one,' he boasted, and was immediately surrounded by a small group of excited young partygoers.

'You know you mentioned dessert?' Russ said slowly. 'Now the pie's gone down I could maybe manage a bit of something.'

'Trifle? Carrot cake?' Angela leapt to her feet.

'Sit down,' Russ hissed, grasping her hand so hard she winced.

'Why?'

'Don't draw attention to yourself.'

'What?'

'Do you like chocolate?'

'I love it.'

'So do I and I think I've found another egg. Would it be against the rules if we bagged it?'

'You've found one. Where?'

'Under the bench. I've just kicked it.'

'I don't think Mum set an age limit. Let's go for it.'

'That's what I was hoping you'd say.' Russ grinned and stooping down, retrieved the Belgian egg and began to peel off the foil. 'There you go. Open wide.'

Russ popped some dark chocolate into her mouth. Angela closed her eyes as the confection melted on her tongue.

'So this is where you're hiding out.'

Angela swallowed her chocolate too quickly and began to cough.

'You'll put on weight and develop spots if you eat too much chocolate,' Judith sniped at her.

'We haven't started on the soft centres yet,' Russ replied. 'Want one?'

'English chocolate? No way.' Judith stepped back as if she had been scalded.

'It's Belgian actually, but if you don't want any, that means there's all the more for us.'

Judith's interpretation of casual dress was an elegant oatmeal shift that showed off her figure to perfection. She looked as though she had never touched a piece of chocolate in her life.

Jack joined the little group.

'Your mother is about to cut her cake, Angela.'

'Cake too?' Judith's expression suggested the party had sunk to unbelievable depths. 'I'm sorry we can't stay for the ceremony. Jack and I have plans for the rest of the day.' Judith linked arms with him.

'I'd better be leaving too.' Russ's expression betrayed nothing as he stood up. 'Thank your mother for the lovely party, Angela. Glad she liked the bookcase.'

The sun disappeared behind a cloud. Angela shivered and the egg she had been holding slipped out of her fingers onto the flagstones and shattered into small pieces.

9

'Now, children, settle down please.' Mrs Potter clapped her hands for attention then smiled at the class of expectant young faces all looking up at her. 'We have two new arrivals this summer term and I want you to give them a real St Andrew's welcome.'

There was a scraping back of chairs as they all stood up and following Mrs Potter's example began to clap as Angela led a shy Mikey into the classroom. Spotting Harry Wilkes sitting in the front row, Mikey grinned at the new friend he had made at Isobel's birthday party.

'Everybody sit down while I introduce our newcomers to you. First we have Michel Stretton.'

'Mikey,' he interrupted, 'my name's Mikey.'

Mrs Potter put a finger to her lips

indicating she wasn't to be interrupted and Angela put a gentle hand on his shoulder to restrain him. Although she hadn't seen much of him during the holidays she had a feeling that like all young boys, now he was getting settled into his new surroundings he might turn into a bit of a handful.

'Mikey is joining us from France, so I expect when we have our sharing information days he will be able to tell us all about his school there.'

Harry's hand shot up.

'Please, Mrs Potter, can Mikey sit next to me?'

'Very well. Go and join your friend, Mikey.'

He scampered across and joined Harry at his painting table.

'Now our second newcomer is a very important lady.' Angela began to feel a little self-conscious as Mrs Potter began to sing her praises. 'As you know, at the end of last term, Mr Harris retired.'

'We had a big party for him,' one of the children said.

'That's right, Katie, we did. Well, his replacement is going to be Miss Banks. She has very kindly agreed to join us this term so we can all get to know each other, and then hopefully from September she will return as the new head teacher of the junior wing of St Andrew's. Won't that be nice?'

The children subjected Angela to a sea of curious glances.

'Miss Banks?' Mrs Potter invited her. 'Perhaps you'd like to say a few words?'

Angela stepped forward. Sun was pouring through the large window at the back of the room. Spring had now well and truly arrived. There was a smell of mown grass from the far field and she couldn't help thinking how different St Andrew's was from her last placing. St Andrew's looked onto open countryside and Mr Harris seemed to have followed a traditional regime of fresh air, lots of time outside to explore the local countryside and a policy of everyone helping everyone else.

'Thank you for that lovely welcome,'

she said, smiling at the children. 'I'm sure with your help Mikey and I will soon feel at home.'

After a brief introduction when she told the children a few things about her plans for the summer term, Mrs Potter left the room and Angela set the children to the task of drawing a picture of something they had seen or done during the Easter break. Keeping a watchful eye over them, she tried to work out which children would be the quieter ones and who could possibly disrupt the smooth flowing of her class.

She didn't have to wait long. While her back was turned there was a loud crash.

'Harry,' Katie wailed, 'you did that on purpose.'

Felt pens rolled in all directions as with much giggling the children began picking them up. Angela waited for them to finish, before curious eyes were turned in her direction to see what she was going to do.

'Would everyone sit down please,' she said in a calm firm voice, knowing this was going to be her first test of authority. The children did as they were told then waited for her to speak again.

'Harry,' she addressed the tousle-haired boy. His school tie had already worked loose from its collar and his socks were down by his ankles.

'Yes, miss?' His eyes were bright with anticipation.

'Come here and bring me your drawing.'

After a moment's hesitation he dragged his feet towards Angela. She inspected his drawing.

'You don't seem to have finished your picture.' Angela held it up for the rest of the class to see. There were one or two sniggers as all Harry had drawn was a circle. 'Perhaps you could tell us what it is supposed to represent?'

'It's an egg,' Harry mumbled, looking at the floor.

'You're going to have to speak up.'

'He said it was an egg, Angela,'

Mikey piped up.

'When we are in class, Mikey, you must address me as Miss Banks,' she admonished him.

'Sorry.' It was Mikey's turn to look chastened.

'He's new,' Harry rushed to his friend's defence, 'he didn't know.'

'In that case,' Angela said, 'would you like to look after him for me, Harry? I'm sure I can trust you to make sure Mikey settles in and show him how things work at St Andrew's.'

'Could do I suppose,' Harry shrugged.

'That's good. Now we've had enough disruption for one morning. So why don't you go and sit down and finish painting your egg for me? I seem to remember you found a purple one in my mother's garden. Why don't you colour it in?'

Relieved to have won her first test of authority, Angela was pleased the rest of the session passed peacefully; and the exercise proved a worthwhile one, with many of the children displaying imaginative pictures of how they had spent their Easter break.

'How are you getting on?' Mrs Potter asked as they supervised the children in the playground at lunchtime.

'Harry Wilkes could be a ringleader stirring things up.'

'He's a good boy with a sense of responsibility at heart,' Mrs Potter replied.

'I asked him to help look after Mikey Stretton.'

'He does seem to be taking his duties seriously doesn't he?' Mrs Potter laughed at the sight of the two boys trying to score goals with a rather flat ball and a decidedly wonky set of goal posts lodged against a wall in the far corner of the playground.

The day passed without any more significant challenges, and when the bell rang at half past three most of the children thanked Angela for a nice day. In the cloakroom she helped them into their coats, located misplaced bags then escorted them outside before going to speak to the small knot of mothers at the gate.

'How are you settling in?' one of them asked Angela.

'As first days go it was quite good,' she said carefully. Experience had taught her not to be too forthcoming when children were around. They always heard what they weren't supposed to and an unguarded remark could have repercussions.

'Katie's given you a good report.' Her mother smiled down at the little girl who was clutching her Easter picture of a trip to the beach.

'I liked today,' she announced. 'Harry knocked over my jar of pens but Miss Banks made him pick them up.'

Her mother raised her eyes in sympathy with Angela. 'I don't envy you the task of looking after that one. He's the youngest of four boys and their parents have rather let them run wild. I think the poor mother ran out of energy by the time Harry was born.'

As the mothers drifted away Angela was aware of a disturbance by the makeshift goalposts.

'Who's there?' she called out.

'Only me, Miss Banks,' a voice replied.

'Mikey? What are you doing?'

'I'm waiting to be collected.'

'You did tell your grandmother school finishes at three-thirty?'

'*Maman* said she would pick me up but I think she forgot,' he said as he carried on kicking his ball. 'Shall I walk home on my own?'

'That is something you must promise me you will never do. It is school policy for you to wait until someone collects you. Do you know where your mother is?'

'Out with Uncle Jack.'

'I thought I heard voices.' Mrs Potter approached. 'Do we have a problem?'

'Can you keep an eye on Mikey?' Angela asked. 'His mother hasn't collected him. I need to call Jacob's Bluff.'

'Use the telephone in the office,' Mrs Potter said.

The telephone rang out for a long time before someone eventually answered.

'Russ? It's Angela.'

'Sorry I took so long; I was in the studio and Ma's out.' He sounded breathless. 'Is something wrong?'

'It's Mikey.'

'What's happened to him?'

'Judith was supposed to collect him from school at three-thirty.' Angela glanced at the clock on the desk. 'It's now five past four.'

Russ groaned. 'She hasn't turned up?'

'Mikey said something about her going out for the day with Jack.'

'I'll be right over. Can you stay with him until I get there?'

'Any luck?' Mrs Potter was gamely standing in goal doing her best to fend off Mikey's attempts to get the ball past her.

'Russ, Mr Stretton I mean, is coming to collect Mikey.'

'Why don't you stand in goal for a bit, Miss Banks,' Mrs Potter suggested, 'while I look out for Mr Stretton?'

'You're not a very good goalkeeper either,' Mikey complained as yet again the ball sailed past Angela's ear, hitting the wall before falling to the ground.

'That's because you're such a good shot.' Angela picked up the ball and tried to bounce it.

'It's flat.' Mikey looked disconsolate.

'I have a pump on my bicycle.'

'I saw your bike. It's by the gates isn't it?'

'Mikey, no, wait,' Angela called after him as he headed in the direction of the road.

'Hey, where's the fire?' Russ laughed as he scooped Mikey up in his arms.

'I've been playing football with Mrs Potter and Miss Banks, but the ball is flat so we were going to get a pump,' Mikey said all in one breath. 'There's one on Miss Banks's bike.'

'You can tell me all about it later.' Russ lowered him to the ground. 'But you mustn't run outside the school gates. Remember your road drill. Now I need to have a quick word with Miss Banks.'

'Come along, Mikey.' Mrs Potter held out her hand. 'Let's go and get your coat and bag.'

'Sorry,' Angela apologised, 'I don't think he would have run into the road, but it's lucky you were there.'

Russ didn't seem to be paying attention to what she was saying. His eyes roamed the playground while Angela experienced a silly urge to pick the wood shavings out of his hair.

'Mikey's had a good first day, as you heard, and he's made a new friend — Harry Wilkes, you remember him? He was at the Easter egg party.' She raised her voice, wondering if she was getting through to Russ.

'Where is Judith?' he demanded.

Angela stiffened. 'I don't know.'

'I can't believe it's happening all over again, Judith forgetting to pick Mikey up after school.'

'Look, Russ, I know it's none of my business,' Angela took a deep breath, 'but you are going to have to work something out with Judith. Whatever issues there are between you, as parents it's your joint responsibility to make sure someone collects Mikey. Russ?' she prompted when he didn't respond.

'I think Judith wants us all to return to France,' he said slowly, 'and this may be her way of saying things would be better in Paris.'

'That's outrageous.' Angela was appalled. 'She can't use a child as a bargaining chip.'

'I wouldn't say she would go that far,' Russ admitted, 'but she can be very devious.'

'Are you planning on returning to France?' Angela asked, intrigued.

'It's not an option.' Russ's voice was firm. 'Anyway, Miss Banks,' he emphasised her title, 'it was your first day at school too. How did you get on?'

'It's a change from my last teaching post,' Angela admitted, 'but it's good.'

'Mrs Potter says to tell you she'll lock up.' Still doing up the buttons of his coat and almost tripping over his schoolbag, Mikey skipped towards them. 'Can we have tea at your house, Angela? Grandma's at a meeting.'

'Mikey,' Russ remonstrated, 'manners — and it's Miss Banks not Angela.'

'You only have to call her Miss Banks during school time,' Mikey explained seriously. 'Outside you can call her Angela. Isn't that right?' the child asked with a worried frown.

Angela laughed. 'You've got it in one. Now,' she confided, 'my mother was baking all day yesterday and I happen to know she tried out a new chocolate cake recipe. Shall we test it to see if it's up to standard?'

Mikey did his best to kick his flat football into the air. 'Can we borrow your bicycle pump too?' he asked as it landed with a flop.

'Only if you help me load the bike into the back of the van,' Russ stipulated.

'I'll tell Mrs Stretton where you've gone shall I?' Mrs Potter called after them. 'If she should turn up before I leave?'

'I would be grateful,' Russ replied, 'but don't stay on specially.'

He reversed his van into the school entrance and between them, he and Mikey picked up Angela's bike. If Judith did appear before Mrs Potter departed for the day, Angela couldn't help feeling she would have chalked up another black mark by taking Mikey and Russ home to tea.

10

'It appears my mother is out.' Angela did a quick check of the downstairs rooms at Wagstaffs Cottage.

'Does that mean we don't get any tea?' Mikey clutched his father's hand as they hovered on the doorstep.

Russ pulled a face. 'Sorry yet again.'

'Look, why don't we just stop apologising to each other?' Angela responded. 'Whether my mother is here or not the invitation still stands.'

'I'll get the cake,' Mikey volunteered.

'I'll get the cake,' Russ corrected him. 'You fetch Angela's bike out of the van and then have a go at blowing up your football with the pump. When you've done that, go into the garden and see if you can organise us somewhere to sit.'

'Got it.' Mikey dashed outside.

'That should keep him occupied for a

while.' Russ brushed his hands off against his jumper and watched in dismay as a shower of sawdust floated to the floor. 'I'm making a mess. Wood shavings will keep following me about. Have you got a brush?'

'Don't worry about it. We gave up being house-proud a long time ago and until you've been plastered from top to toe in play paint you are an amateur when it comes to looking a mess.'

'Think I'll give that one a miss.' Russ finished rubbing himself down.

'Come and see. What do you think? It's in pride of place.' Angela pushed open the sitting-room door. The book-case now stood against a far wall. 'We've had loads of compliments and enquiries.' Angela picked up an envelope bulging with cards and scraps of paper. 'All interested parties.'

Russ accepted the envelope. 'That's brilliant.' He pushed it into the pocket of his cargo pants. 'What can I do for you and Isobel in return?'

'Ten per cent commission?' Angela

raised an eyebrow.

'Ma would have pushed for fifteen.'

'Your mother will never go hungry and I was only joking.'

'Well if you fancy a new chair on the house you know where to come. Um, they do still have one leg at each corner don't they?'

Before Angela could reply a loud thud was followed by the squeaking of bicycle tyres.

'Are you sure Mikey can manage?' She glanced out the window to where the boy was struggling with schoolbag, pump and her bike.

'I'm hoping the extra activity will wear him out.' Russ followed her glance and waved at his son. 'Although I have to be honest, the school football's had it, but we'll let Mikey find that out for himself.'

Angela wished Russ wouldn't smile at her with quite such a degree of warmth. Reminding herself that Judith was still very much a part of his life, she suggested, 'We'd better get on with making the tea.'

She pushed open the kitchen door. The boiler hummed companionably in a corner of the kitchen and the warm air smelt of spices and newly baked bread.

'You'll find the chocolate cake on a cooling rack in the cupboard. I think you'll find some sultana biscuits too. The tin's got a picture of Big Ben on the front.'

'Found it.' Russ placed the tin on the table. 'Now, chocolate cake.' His voice was muffled as he disappeared back into the cupboard. 'What the — ?' He spun round at the noise of water spluttering violently out of the kettle spout. 'Steady, it's going everywhere.'

Turning her attention back to the task in hand, Angela snatched up a sponge and began mopping up the mess on the draining board.

'Wasn't paying attention,' she said by way of explanation.

'Was it something I said?' Russ asked with a frown.

'What?' Angela knew her cheeks had reddened.

'Is something wrong? You're looking flustered.'

'No.' Angela shook her head. 'I'm always doing that.' She attempted a light laugh and flung the sponge into the washing-up bowl.

Russ didn't look convinced by her poor explanation, but how could she explain that watching him perform a task as simple as getting biscuits out of a cupboard had set her pulses racing like they had done when she had been a tiresome teenager who used to trail around after him?

Besides, Russ had already demonstrated that Judith was a significant presence in his life by using Angela as a gooseberry, and role replay was not on her agenda.

Mentally lecturing herself to get a life, Angela asked, 'How's Pauline?' She began wiping down the kettle then placing it on the base before flicking the switch.

'Her hip's troublesome, but she wouldn't thank me for telling you.' Russ deftly placed the chocolate cake on one of the plates Angela passed across the table. 'Otherwise, she is fine. Mission accomplished.' He stood back to admire his handiwork, then sniffed. 'Scones?'

'I don't know about you but I forgot lunch.' Angela retrieved the batch she had quickly slipped into the oven. She waved her butter knife at Russ, threatening to topple the mountain of warm scones.

'Do you think I've done enough?'

Russ inspected the loaded tray.

'Are you sure my son ate his dinner?'

'Fish fingers, chips and peas, and jelly with peach slices to follow.'

'Then he can't be hungry.'

'Small boys are always hungry. You carry the tray. I'll bring the drinks.'

A disconsolate Mikey was standing in the middle of the lawn, clutching the bicycle pump.

'No luck?' Russ nodded towards the

deflated football.

'All it does it make a horrid noise when I try to fill it with air.'

His crestfallen expression evaporated as he spotted the chocolate cake on the table.

'Can I have a piece?' He wriggled onto one of the garden seats.

Angela cut him a slice and poured out some orange juice then nudged the plate of scones towards Russ.

'How did it go today?' Russ began coating a scone with raspberry jam.

'Brilliant.' Mikey giggled between bites of chocolate cake. 'We drew pictures. Harry's wasn't very good.'

'That's not a nice thing to say,' Russ chided his son.

'It's true isn't it, Angela?' Mikey turned to her for support. 'You said his egg was silly.'

'I said no such thing,' Angela insisted, making a mental note not to disparage Harry in front of the class again. 'Why don't you show your father your picture?'

Mikey snatched up his dropped school bag and withdrew a crumpled sheet of paper. Russ flattened it out on the garden table.

'Very good.' He inspected his son's efforts then pointed to a red-skinned figure with a shock of unkempt hair, wearing violently green bathing shorts. 'Who's that?'

'It's you,' Mikey explained. 'I know your shorts were blue but Harry was using the blue pen. It's the day we spent on the beach. That's me there and that's *Maman*. I couldn't put Angela in because she'd gone back to the van.'

Russ's eyes met Angela's over Mikey's head.

'Would you like some more juice, Mikey?' Angela asked.

'Please.'

The table wobbled as he leapt up and thrust his empty glass at her.

'Why don't you have another go at blowing up the football?' Russ suggested to his son. 'Angela and I need to talk.'

'Is there any more chocolate cake, please?' Mikey asked, licking up some stray crumbs off his plate with his wet finger.

'Only a small bit,' Russ insisted, 'otherwise you'll get tummy ache.'

Clutching his second slice of cake, Mikey raced off down the garden. Russ pushed away his jam-smeared plate and watched Angela fill up their teacups.

'Finished?' he asked with a trace of amusement. 'Didn't want to disturb you in case the sound of my voice made you spill more hot water.'

Angela put down the teapot. Russ leaned across the table towards her. His breath was warm against her face as he said in a quiet voice, 'We need to talk about Judith.'

'I don't want to talk about her behind her back,' Angela insisted.

'I'm not asking you to tell tales,' Russ said, 'but you're close to Jack Brewer, aren't you?'

'He looks after my mother's car and he has helped her with her computer skills.' Angela did her best to sound casual.

'I wondered if he'd mentioned Judith at all.'

'He hasn't said a thing.' Angela didn't see she had any reason to tell Russ she had hardly seen Jack since her mother's Easter egg party.

'I can't help feeling she is up to something,' Russ said.

'Like what?'

Russ picked at a stray shaving of wood on his jumper then twisted it round his fingers.

'You saw the disruption she caused today.'

The intimacy of this discussion was making Angela feel uncomfortable and she wasn't sure she wanted to continue.

'When we lived in Paris Judith's mother helped out as much as she could but Madeleine has a job.' It was as though Russ was now speaking to himself. 'And if we return to France, the situation will be exactly the same. It won't have changed and it's not a risk

I'm prepared to take.'

'You could employ an agent.'

'I'm not keen on that idea either.'

'Then that only leaves Madeleine.'

'I don't think Judith would ask for her mother's help.'

'Why not?'

'Madeline was not sympathetic to Judith's cause. She felt her daughter was in the wrong when she didn't collect Mikey from school. They had words and ever since then their relationship has been cool.'

'It can't have been an easy situation for Judith.'

Russ looked at Angela in surprise.

'That's a very generous comment.'

'I'd be lost without my career so I can appreciate Judith's side of things.'

'Can you? What would you think about her wanting to take Mikey back to France?'

Angela bit her lip. Sentiment was all very well, but when it came to influencing the lives of those around you, she wasn't so sure it was such a good thing.

'It's something you and Judith must sort out, but speaking as his teacher I would say now he's started his new school it would be nice if he could enjoy a period of stability.'

'I agree. He's settled here. You are his teacher. He likes and trusts you. Then there's my mother. She absolutely dotes on him. He's found new friends. He doesn't need any more disruption.'

The sun's rays highlighted Russ's unkempt hair, a deep chestnut.

'You forgot to shave this morning.' Angela resisted the temptation to run a finger down the side of his face.

'Actually,' he confessed, 'I was drying out some varnish on a chair and I had two heaters going full blast so when I plugged in my razor I overloaded the system and fused the lights. Ma was not best pleased. By the time I'd run up the drive to the main house she was busy giving the power company a bit of an earful. I had to race round resetting the trip and when I finished I'd forgotten what I'd been doing in the first place.

All in all this morning was a bit of a disaster.'

Russ fumbled self-consciously with a loose thread on his jumper. Angela couldn't help noticing his hands were ingrained with oil and bore scarred evidence of where his carving chisel had slipped and nicked his fingers.

'What are you looking at now?' he asked.

'Your work-stained hands.'

Angela knew her grown-up feelings for Russ were foolish in the extreme. He was using her to get back at Judith, who was more than capable of claiming that Angela had abused her position as Mikey's teacher by entering into a relationship with his father.

Russ slid his hand across the garden table.

'Papa,' Mikey trilled, 'I've drawn a picture of Angela 'cos I left her out of the last one.'

Tearing his eyes away from Angela's, Russ glanced at the picture Mikey thrust under his nose.

'That's very good.'

'You're paddling in the sea with Angela and she's holding your hand. Are you listening to me, Papa?' he demanded. 'I saw you together hand in hand in the sea so I thought I'd draw a picture of it. Do you like it? I saw you kissing Angela too but I'm not very good at drawing kisses.'

Russ didn't reply. He was looking over his son's shoulder. Angela spun round.

'Mrs Potter said I'd find you here.'

The coldness in Judith's voice matched the expression in her eyes.

'Hello Judith,' Russ greeted her casually. 'What kept you from collecting our son from school this time?' he enquired.

159

11

'You needn't think you can worm your way into my husband's heart via Mikey,' Judith hissed, 'and a slice of chocolate cake.'

Aware of the curious glances being cast in their direction by some of the mothers at the school gate, Angela drew Judith to one side.

'I'm not trying to,' she explained, 'and will you please keep your voice down, you're disturbing the children.'

'It won't do you any good telling tales either.' Judith looked in no mood to keep her voice down.

'What do you mean?' Angela demanded.

'About Jack and me.'

When the two of them had turned up at Wagstaffs Cottage the tea party had broken up. After a cursory glance at the picture Mikey had drawn of Angela and Russ holding hands in the sea, Judith had thrust it into Mikey's school bag, her expression one of distaste.

'Jack has offered to be my driver while I'm over here. I don't have a car and as I don't like driving on the left it's an arrangement that suits us both, and that's why I didn't pick Mikey up the other day. I didn't forget. Jack and I got delayed by road works.'

'You could have left a message.'

'I couldn't get a signal on my mobile.'

'Whatever, your private life is none of my business,' Angela insisted.

'Can you imagine how I felt when I arrived at the school to find that woman locking up and no sign of my son?'

Judith pointed to where the deputy head teacher was tidying up the playground.

'You kept Mrs Potter waiting over an hour. She has her own family to consider and it was very generous of her to stay on.'

Angela was staunch in her defence of her colleague but nothing seemed to stop Judith's flow.

'I had no idea where Mikey was.'

'He was safe with me and his father and Mrs Potter informed you of our whereabouts, so if you had a problem with that it was of your own making.'

Judith tossed back her head in a gesture of dismissal.

'If I report you to the authorities, your job could be on the line.'

'You must do as you think fit, Judith.'

'My name is Mrs Stretton.'

'Then if you'll excuse me, Mrs Stretton, I have my duties to attend to.'

'One more thing.' She put out a hand to detain Angela. 'I'm giving you formal notice that as soon as I can arrange things Mikey and I are moving back to France.'

'Is it wise to uproot him again?' Angela asked in a calmer voice, anxious not to inflame the situation.

'I'll be the best judge of that.'

'He is settling down well. He's a bright child and you can visit whenever you like.'

The moment she spoke Angela knew she had said the wrong thing.

'I don't need you to tell me when I can visit my own son thank you very much.'

Judith's reaction was very much what Angela would have expected.

'That isn't what I meant.'

Before Angela could attempt to put things right they were interrupted by a new arrival.

'Hello girls.' Jack strolled towards them. 'Had a bit of trouble finding somewhere to park. I had no idea the school run was such big business. It's solid all the way down the road.'

Judith's expression lightened at the sound of his voice.

'There you are. We're ready, aren't we, Mikey?' She tugged her son's hand.

'Can Harry come to tea?' he asked.

'Not today. Uncle Jack and I have some business to attend to.'

'Can I go to tea with Angela? She does scrummy cakes.'

'I told you not today,' Judith insisted.

'You can have Harry to tea another time. Sorry,' she mouthed to Harry's mother who was hovering nearby.

'Perhaps Mikey would like to come to us?' Mrs Wilkes suggested. ''Fraid you'll have to take us as you find us. My catering is not up to Miss Banks's standards.'

'No one measures up to Miss Banks,' Judith replied with a smile that didn't reach her eyes, 'when it comes to cakes.'

'Yes, well,' Mrs Wilkes gave the little group a flustered smile, 'another time perhaps. Come along, Harry. Mikey's busy today.'

'How are things with you, Angela?' Jack asked, his smile easing the tension. 'I haven't been round to visit lately, I've been tied up with other things.'

Judith linked a possessive arm through Jack's.

'Angela doesn't have time for a social life these days apart from the occasional tea party with my son and ex-husband.'

Another parent anxious to attract her attention saved Angela from replying.

Moments later the playground was deserted, the silence punctuated by the whining of the wire gate as it swung on its hinges. Picking up a stray piece of litter, Angela dropped the drinks can in the bin as the gate crashed open and Russ burst through.

'I'm not late am I?' he gasped.

'What are you doing here?'

'Where is everyone?'

'They've gone home.'

'I've come to pick up Mikey.'

'Judith collected him.'

'What?'

'She was with Jack Brewer.'

'When was this?'

'About ten minutes ago.'

Russ stifled a muffled curse and ran a hand through his windswept hair.

'How did that happen?'

'Look, Russ.' Angela was beginning to feel if she never saw another member of the Stretton family, it would be too soon. 'You and Judith are going to have to get to grips with the school run. Mrs Potter and I have other children to look

165

after besides Mikey. If you give us a list at the beginning of the week telling us whose day it is to pick him up, we'll stick to it. If you could manage to do that, Russ?'

He was looking up and down the road outside as if expecting to see Mikey running towards him.

'Did you know Judith intends going back to France?'

'She did mention it.'

'You remember that boardroom commission I was telling you about?'

'The one for the stud farm?' Angela frowned at the abrupt change of subject.

'They want me to inspect their premises, to get a feel of the place. They are holding an open day and I've been invited along.'

'Where's this going, Russ?' Angela enquired.

'I've also been invited to stay over for preliminary discussions. I can't afford to say no to such an opportunity.'

'And this would be?'

'Next week.'

'Then who will be collecting Mikey?'

'I'll arrange something with my mother. You needn't worry about Ma forgetting, she's as reliable as clock-work.'

'Fine.' Angela picked up the gate key that had fallen out of her fingers when Russ had collided with her.

'You've done something to your hair.' Russ put out a hand as if to touch it, then let it drop by his side.

'I've had it trimmed.' Angela fingered the back of her neck in a self-conscious gesture. It felt bare and she was still getting used to her new cropped style. 'It's easier to have it like this when dealing with a class full of excited youngsters.'

'So it wasn't for Jack Brewer's benefit?'

'I've explained why I had it cut.' Angela bridled at the assumption that she would change her hairstyle for the likes of Jack Brewer. 'And it has absolutely nothing to do with Jack.'

'Judith was telling me how he isn't always available to drive her around because he's with you.'

'The only time Jack drove me anywhere was because I had a puncture on my bicycle. Actually no, that's not true. If you remember he came to collect me at Jacob's Bluff but Mikey fell off the swing and Jack wound up taking him and Judith to the doctor. You can't have forgotten. I got the blame? In fact I seem to get the blame for everything that goes wrong in your life.'

'What about the Easter egg party?'

'What about it?'

'Jack was being very helpful.'

'Yes, he was and again if you remember, he left the party with Judith, not with me. But even if he hadn't, I don't have to justify my actions to you. I can go out with anyone I like.'

'Not with Jack Brewer you can't.'

'I beg your pardon?' Angela could hardly believe what she was hearing.

'He's got a reputation.'

'This conversation ends right now,' Angela insisted. 'The sooner you get your act together with Judith, the better. Now if you don't mind I have a busy evening ahead of me finishing off my thesis.'

With a firm thrust of the gate, Angela turned the key in the lock leaving Russ on the other side of the fence. Not bothering to turn round to see if he was watching her, she strode back into the empty classrooms.

* * *

'Angela, dear? Is that you?'

'Pauline?' Angela was in the head teacher's office completing her day's report.

'I know it's an awful imposition,' she began.

'What time will you be picking Mikey up? Classes finished at three-thirty and,' she glanced at the clock on the desk, 'it's now twenty to four.'

'That's just it. I can't make it.'

Angela stifled a sigh of annoyance. So much for Russ's mother being as regular as clockwork.

'My appointment over ran and I've only this instant got back.'

'I've some paperwork to catch up on so I can hang on here a little while.'

'That won't be necessary, dear. I've ordered a taxi from a reputable company I use all the time. The only thing is . . . ' Pauline hesitated. ' . . . the driver is new and naturally reluctant to pick up a child who doesn't know him. He doesn't know Mikey either and I was wondering would you mind terribly bringing him home in the taxi? You can put your bicycle in the boot can't you?'

Angela closed her eyes in exasperation.

'Angela?' Pauline prompted when she didn't immediately reply.

'Very well,' Angela agreed, professionalism getting the better of her personal feelings. 'We'll be with you shortly.'

Mikey could barely contain his excitement as he bounced around in the back of the cab.

'I've never been in a taxi before,' he confided. '*Maman* won't let us use them in Paris. She says they are too expensive.'

'Sit still,' Angela admonished him. 'We don't want to cause an accident.'

'Grandma's been to the hospital,' Mikey confided. 'She's going to have a peration.'

'A what?' Angela demanded.

'On her hip. It hurt last week so we couldn't play cricket. She fell asleep in the afternoon.' Mikey put a hand to his mouth in a gesture of horror. 'I wasn't supposed to tell anyone.'

'The fare's already been seen to, madam,' the driver interrupted as they drew up outside Jacob's Bluff.

'Thank you very much,' Mikey trilled to the driver as he jumped out of the vehicle.

Pauline was waiting for them on the steps.

'This is so good of you, Angela.'

To Angela's surprise the older woman gave her a kiss on the cheek.

'It's my wretched hip again.'

'Mikey said something about an operation?' Angela queried. Pauline Stretton was of a generation that never went to bed during the day and Mikey's revelation had shocked her.

'Come in and have some tea. I can offer you some cake courtesy of your mother. Mikey, would you like to watch television while you have yours? Watching television during meal times is not something I would normally encourage,' she said in an aside to Angela, 'but I need to talk to you.'

Angela settled down in the elegant drawing room Pauline liked to use to entertain her guests.

'Judith has returned to France, did you know?'

'Already? I thought she was taking Mikey with her.'

'It's only a temporary arrangement. A family matter needed her attention. She will be back but that's not what I want to talk to you about. Frankly I think she and Jack Brewer are up to something. It can't have escaped your notice how close they have become.'

'You needn't worry about Jack. He isn't looking to settle down. You know as well as I do what he's like — footloose and fancy free.'

'What if Judith made it worth his while?'

'To do what?' Angela asked, puzzled.

'To help her abscond?'

'With Mikey?'

'Yes.'

'Why would she need to do that? Russ wouldn't stand in her way.'

'I'm not so sure.' Pauline looked unconvinced. 'He feels quite strongly that Mikey should stay here now he's settled.'

Angela shook her head. 'Jack would never be party to such an arrangement. I really think you have no cause to worry on that score.'

'I took a telephone call a few days

ago from France. Judith wasn't here so the caller left a message. She has come into an inheritance from an uncle who has a château in the Loire Valley. You can see where this might lead?'

'She's going to be a woman of property?'

'If that is the case she would have no need to rely on her mother's help. They have had a slight falling out over Mikey, I gather, and Madeleine Grange said she could no longer help with his care. But if Judith is financially independent then she could make her own arrangements.'

Pauline looked tired as she leaned back against her cushion. A flash of annoyance prevented Angela from saying what she thought of the situation. Pauline did not need this and neither did she.

'Did you tell Russ about the call from France?'

'He wasn't here at the time and then I got to thinking about it and decided not to. I don't know why really.'

'Then why are you telling me?'

'It helps to have someone to talk to. Have you come across this type of situation before?'

'It isn't unique,' Angela admitted, 'but you must talk to Russ, the sooner the better. He has to know.' She held up a hand to forestall the older woman. 'I will not do the job for you, Pauline.'

'You're quite right and it was unfair of me to consider the idea,' she replied, 'but discussing it with you has helped me see things more clearly. Thank you. Now let's talk about something else. How is Mikey settling in at school?'

Pauline nudged a small portion of cake around her plate. Angela noticed she hadn't eaten very much.

'He has palled up with a boy called Harry Wilkes.'

Pauline pulled a face.

'He came to tea the other day. A rather boisterous child who knocked over an antique vase.'

'That sounds like Harry,' Angela sympathised.

'More tea?'

Pauline almost dropped the pot as a streak of lightning split the sky followed moments later by a loud crash of thunder. Rain began to lash at the window.

'Goodness, what on earth is happening?'

'It's been threatening all day. The children were very restless this afternoon. I think the pressure was getting to them. I'd better get home,' Angela replied, 'before the back way floods.'

'You can't cycle in this. Take my car,' Pauline insisted. 'I won't be needing it for a day or two. You'll be covered by the insurance.'

Hailstones pounded the window with such force Angela was worried the glass would crack.

'Mikey,' Pauline called him over. 'Come and say goodbye to Miss Banks. She's leaving.'

The little boy abandoned his television programme and running across the room threw his arms round Angela's neck. His body was sturdy against hers — a contrast to the pale thin child who had arrived from Paris, almost too nervous to speak.

'What time are you picking me up tomorrow morning in Grandma's car?' he asked.

12

Isobel was peering anxiously out of the front door of Wagstaffs as Angela splashed the tyres of Pauline's car through the puddles. Unused to the automatic controls and careful not to exceed any speed limits, Angela had driven slowly and the journey had taken much longer than usual. Brilliant sunshine had now replaced the rain, dazzling Angela for the last part of her drive.

'I was about to send out a search party,' Isobel greeted her daughter in relief. 'Where have you been? You're very late.'

'Pauline didn't collect Mikey from school.' Angela clambered out of the driving seat after parking the car on the greensward.

'Where's your bicycle and why are you driving Pauline Stretton's car?'

'Mind if I have a shower first?' Angela grabbed her bag from the back seat. Her bicycle, she decided, could stay in the boot for the moment.

'Supper in half an hour?' Isobel suggested. 'I've done us a casserole. I expect you skipped lunch? I don't know what it is with you young people. No one eats properly any more.'

'There isn't time to eat lunch when you've got hoards of excited children to keep an eye on. Someone's always falling down or getting into a fight.'

'Go freshen up.' Isobel stroked her daughter's hair. 'I'll see to the casserole. Fancy a glass of wine?'

'Mm, that sounds lovely.'

Angela inspected her reflection in the mirror as she blow-dried her hair. She hadn't had that much cut off but she had been surprised that Russ should have noticed. Apart from Mrs Potter no one else had. Fluffing her hair into shape she turned the nozzle to the cool setting and finished off. She supposed it was too much to hope that a class full of five-year-olds would notice any change in their teacher's appearance.

'Supper's ready,' Isobel called up the stairs.

'Coming,' Angela called back, shrugging on a tee shirt and a fresh skirt and applying a quick squirt of perfume before heading downstairs.

The sound of muffled voices drew her towards the kitchen. Isobel hadn't mentioned anything about visitors but her mother operated an open house policy and unexpected guests were not an unusual occurrence at Wagstaffs.

'There you are.' Isobel looked up from the oven. 'We've one extra for dinner.'

'Jack.' Angela greeted him with a kiss.

'Hope you don't mind. I called by on the off chance of catching you at home and your mother insisted I stay for a bite to eat.'

'Yet another one who missed out on lunch.' Isobel cast Jack a disapproving look.

'I worked through. I've rather let the

paperwork slip,' he admitted. 'I had a backlog of bills and invoices to get out. If you don't keep on top of things it soon mounts up.'

'This lapse wouldn't be anything to do with Judith would it?' Angela enquired with a sweet smile.

'Carry the vegetables through will you, Angela?' Isobel indicated a serving dish and a pair of oven gloves, at the same time giving her daughter a look that indicated whatever Jack got up to with Judith, it was none of their business.

'Let me,' Jack insisted.

'Careful then, it's hot,' Isobel warned.

'And don't drop it,' Angela put in, 'or you'll be very unpopular.'

'Jack is our guest,' Isobel said in her no-nonsense voice as she handed Angela the potatoes.

'Doesn't give him the right to drop the vegetables,' Angela retaliated, not in the least abashed by her mother's reprimand. 'I don't know about you but I'm not keen on eating broccoli off the floor.'

'Get on with you before it gets cold,' Isobel chided her.

Jack proved an entertaining dinner guest relating stories of life on the garage floor.

'I thought I was going mad when tyre nuts kept going missing and spanners began going astray for no apparent reason. Then after one of the mechanics accused another of stealing his lunch-time sandwiches, I knew I had to act before I had a riot on my hands.'

'What did you do?' Isobel asked.

'I seriously began to think the place was haunted when some keys went walkabout off my desk. Everyone denied knowing anything about any of the incidents. I was on the verge of calling in the police.'

Isobel filled Jack's plate with more potatoes as he paused to sip his wine.

'Do you have a resident ghost?' Angela asked.

'It turns out the culprit was next door's dog. All the units are connected and because Boxer is a black Labrador no one really noticed him. He used to sneak in and take things. Poor old Marec was so embarrassed. He's a Polish plumber and he's not always on site. He thought his partner was looking after their dog and the partner thought Boxer was with Marec. It was quite a mix up. Marec found a whole stash of goodies hidden away in his lock-up. He had to go round and apologise to everybody. Still, no harm done. It's a good story to dine out on and this is extremely good casserole, Isobel.' Jack finished his story and wiped his plate clean with the last piece of seeded bread. 'One of your best I'd say. Ever thought of becoming a television chef?'

'I would hate the idea. Now I hope you've got room for lemon meringue pie?'

'If there's one thing I never can resist it is lemon meringue pie, although I may have to undo my belt a notch. Perhaps a small slice?'

Jack was doing what he liked best, charming the ladies; and Angela had to admit he was good at it, which made it all the more impossible to believe he could be involved in anything shady with Judith. He may have sailed close to the wind once or twice with his affairs of the heart, but she was convinced that would be as far as his transgressions would go.

After the lemon meringue pie had been demolished and they were left looking at an empty dish, Isobel stood up.

'I have some admin of my own to catch up on,' she explained, 'and now I'm computer literate due to excellent instruction, I want to update my statistics. Help yourself to coffee.'

'You load the dishwasher,' Angela instructed Jack as she piled up the plates, 'then we'll have coffee outside. After all that rain it's turned into a lovely evening.'

They watched the setting sun disappear behind the horizon in companionable silence, Angela remembering the beach sunset she had enjoyed with Russ before they indulged in mugs of hot chocolate in Stan's café. She wondered how he was getting on in Newmarket and how long he would be away.

'I actually called by,' Jack's voice cut into her thoughts, 'to apologise.'

Angela drew her attention back to the present. 'What for?' she asked.

'I know she doesn't mean anything by it but sometimes Judith can be a bit, well, forthright.'

'Only with me it would seem.'

'I think she's insecure.'

'I still don't see that as a reason to be forthright with me.'

'Well, I just thought I'd say sorry. It was my fault we were late picking up Mikey from school the other day. I hadn't realised the time.'

'It's good of you to take the blame.'

'Noble is my middle name,' Jack quipped.

'Can I ask you a question?'

'I don't have to answer it if I don't like it,' Jack replied with his easy smile. 'Fire away.'

'Are you romantically involved with Judith?'

'No, I'm not,' he said slowly. 'Our relationship is purely a business one.'

'Why do you keep going to Norwich?'

'Who told you that?' Jack frowned.

'Russ, I think, or it might have been Mikey.'

'The short answer is we don't. We made plans to have a day out but Judith returned to Paris at short notice to deal with a family matter that had arisen, so we never got there. I've been showing her a bit of the countryside and taking her shopping, that sort of thing, that's all.' He paused. 'My turn now to ask you a question. Was that Pauline Stretton's car I saw parked outside?'

'She's letting me use it because she can't pick Mikey up after school. I've been volunteered into doing the school run while Russ is away.'

'Surely you've enough calls on your time.'

'I agree but have you tried getting the

better of Pauline Stretton? Besides, her hip really is paining her.'

'I could always pick Mikey up in your place. I am a responsible adult and Mikey knows me.'

'You'd better discuss it with Pauline, not me,' Angela replied.

In the distance an owl hooted.

'I think that's my cue to leave, don't you?' Jack finished his coffee. 'By the way there's a new Italian place opened up along the coast. I've heard good reports, if you fancy going out one evening? You don't have to make a decision right now, just something to bear in mind. I promise to be on my best behaviour.'

'Goodness,' Isobel said as she came out onto the terrace, 'I didn't realise you were still here, Jack.'

'Another cue to take my leave I think. Thank you for the most delicious supper I've had in a long time.' He kissed Isobel's hand. 'Let me know about that dinner date,' he said to Angela.

'He mentioned a new Italian restaurant he thought I might like,' Angela explained as he drove off, 'but if you're going to give me the lecture about it not being a good idea to accept his invitation or to go out with him, then I've already had it, from Russ.'

'Have you indeed?'

'And I'll give you the same answer I gave him. I can make my own decisions as to whom I go out with.'

'Perhaps you should accept Jack's invitation. I'm sure he would be good company for the evening.'

'You've changed your tune.' Angela regarded her mother in surprise.

'There's something I think you ought to know.' Isobel locked the French windows and pulled the curtains and switched the table lamps on. 'Sit down.'

Intrigued, Angela perched on the edge of the sofa.

'The Stretton family situation,' Isobel began. 'I can see it getting rather messy and you, my darling, could find yourself involved.'

'I've done nothing to be ashamed of.'

'It doesn't matter. Judith needs a scapegoat and you fit the bill nicely.'

'I think you're fussing unnecessarily.'

'Maybe so but is it true Judith's come into an inheritance?'

'News does travel fast in this part of the world.'

'I thought as much.' Isobel nodded. 'As you know I do not listen to gossip much less repeat it, but Judith would be perfectly within her rights to plead she is better placed than Russ is to look after Mikey. She is his mother. She will have financial independence and unlike his father she is not romantically involved.'

'But none of it's true, I mean the bit about Russ and me being romantically involved.'

'It doesn't matter. It is how Judith will present her cause to anyone who wants to listen. That is why I am warning you to be on your guard. You want this new position as head teacher of the junior wing of St Andrew's don't you?'

'You know I do.'

'Then it's doubly important you do not get involved in any scandal. Surely you can see that? You have to be seen to be above suspicion. People will believe what they want to believe. It's my duty as your mother to tell you what I think.'

A cold lump of dread lodged in Angela's stomach. She knew only too well how word travelled in an enclosed community.

'I would hate you to miss out on the job of a lifetime due to unfounded rumours. That is why it might be a good idea for you to be seen in Jack Brewer's company. I know you're not silly enough to let him break your heart, so next time he asks you out, I would suggest you accept.'

'Did you plan this evening's little get together?'

'No, but when Jack dropped by he played into my hands.' Isobel kissed her daughter's forehead. 'I've said all I've got to say on the subject. Get a good night's sleep. It's amazing how much better you'll feel in the morning.'

Angela made her way upstairs. As usual her mother was right. Judith would make mileage out of any situation if she thought it would further her cause.

Angela stifled a yawn. With the half term holiday coming up next week, she was more than ready for a break.

She turned out the bedroom light, but it was a long time before she fell asleep.

13

'Come along, boys.' Pauline Stretton raised her voice in an effort to attract their attention. 'We're ready to leave.'

'Is Miss Banks coming with us?' a red-faced Harry demanded, his sword fight with Mikey abandoned.

'Not today. Now have we got everything?'

Pauline checked the forecourt then closed the boot of the car.

'In you get.'

'I know the way to the bay,' Mikey announced importantly as the boys scrambled into the back seat. 'I've been down there before.'

'I've been there too,' Harry declared.

'No, you haven't.'

'Yes I have.'

The boys immediately engaged in a tussle that Pauline didn't have the strength to break up. She started the car engine. Her hip ached and she was beginning to question the wisdom of suggesting the half term outing, but Mikey had been growing restless and with both his parents away her grandson needed distraction. Inviting Harry over for the day had been the obvious choice but she hadn't realised he would be such a bundle of energy and she had forgotten that looking after two excited boys was hard work.

'Settle down and do up your seat belts,' she instructed them in her best grandmother's voice.

There was an obedient click from the back seat as Harry snapped his buckle.

'When can we start the picnic?' he asked.

'We've got to find some buried treasure first.' Mikey jabbed his friend in the ribs.

'I don't believe in all that shipwreck stuff,' Harry scoffed.

'You should,' Pauline admonished him.

'Why's that then?' he asked, his eyes

193

bright with anticipation.

'Pirates used to roam these shores in olden days.' Pauline wasn't too sure of her facts but she doubted the boys knew any better and she was fairly certain they wouldn't contradict her. 'Several vessels came to grief during the great storm of seventy-six.' She began to enjoy herself as she entered the spirit of things and her powers of invention got into their stride.

'Nineteen seventy-six?' Mikey asked.

'Seventeen seventy-six,' Pauline corrected him.

History was not her strong point, but again she counted on the boys not knowing much about the eighteenth century, and from the expression on their faces she could see they appeared to accept her word as true.

'Cool,' Mikey replied, a note of awe in his voice.

'All right, then.' Harry gave Mikey a playful punch in the chest. 'Any treasures we find we split down the middle.'

There was a slap as they high-fived.

Pauline's mind wandered onto other matters as the boys began to plan their day.

She hadn't heard from Judith since her return to France and with Russ away too, the demands on her time had been considerable.

Pauline felt rather guilty about the way she had manoeuvred Angela into doing the school run by offering her the use of the car, and that was why she had decided it wasn't fair to impose on her during the half term break.

'Turn left here, Grandma,' Mikey called out.

Preoccupied with her thoughts, Pauline had been about to overshoot.

'Thank you, darling,' she smiled at him and quickly turned the steering wheel. 'Nearly there,' she said brightly as Harry began to fidget in his seat.

'I can see the bay,' he announced, catching her eye in the mirror.

'We can look in the sand for the treasure,' Mikey said. 'It might have been buried for hundreds of years so we'll have to dig deep.'

With so much on her mind Pauline had forgotten her cardinal rule to always check the local timetable before they left Jacob's Bluff. At times it wasn't unknown for the beach to be cut off.

There were rocks where they could take shelter if the worst should happen but it would be a long wait for the tide to turn and the prospect of being marooned didn't bear thinking about. She comforted herself with the thought that two active boys would be able to shin over the dunes before any tide caught up with them. Her hip gave a sharp twinge as if to remind Pauline it wasn't too sure if she'd be able to keep up with them.

Pushing thoughts of fleeing from an incoming tide to the back of her mind, she parked the car away from the brisk breeze blowing off the sea.

Isobel had provided a sturdy picnic hamper that Pauline now handed to the boys.

196

'Be very careful with it, it's our lunch and if you drop it we won't have anything to eat.'

Her words had an immediate effect on Harry and Mikey who proceeded to carry the basket down the dunes as carefully as if it were a baby. She locked the car then followed with the other bits and pieces.

The sun was warm and soon rose high in the sky. While the boys scampered off to explore their surroundings Pauline settled under her sunshade and opened a book, but her head felt heavy and her eyelids began to droop before she had finished the first page.

'Grandma, we're hungry.' Pauline was abruptly woken up by Mikey shaking her arm.

'And I'd like something to drink,' Harry added, spraying sand over her feet as he ran round in circles impersonating an aircraft.

The sun had moved overhead and Pauline was distressed to realise she had been snoozing for over an hour.

Luckily neither of the boys appeared to have noticed or to have suffered from her lack of supervision.

'Have you had any success with your treasure?' she asked, sorting out drinks for everyone.

'Only a two pence piece, some seashells and a crab,' Mikey announced forlornly, then appeared to forget his disappointment as he began to devour banana sandwiches.

'These are fantastic.' Harry finished his second one in as many minutes.

'Want some crisps?' Mikey produced a huge bag and tried to open it.

'Let me, please.' Pauline's offer was too late. The bag split and the contents cascaded onto the beach rug.

Mikey broke into peals of laughter.

'Don't worry, Mrs Stretton,' Harry assured her, 'they won't go to waste. They taste just as good off the rug as off a plate.'

Pauline smiled at him.

'I'm pleased to hear you're not a fussy eater.'

She could see Harry's visit had been exactly the tonic Mikey needed as he began scooping up the crisps before Harry could devour them all. Nibbling on the smoked salmon sandwich that Isobel had thoughtfully provided for her, Pauline looked out to sea. The sun dazzled her eyes and she squinted at the horizon. The tide looked relatively calm but she knew how quickly it could turn and she didn't want to be caught unawares. She decided against asking the boys to carry the basket back to the car now. It would mean entrusting them with the keys and should they drop them in the sand she hadn't got a spare set on her.

'Can we go for a swim?' Mikey asked wiping crisp crumbs from his mouth.

'Not so soon after your lunch,' Pauline replied.

'Why not?' he pouted, crossing his arms as if prepared for confrontation.

'Why don't you play beach cricket?' Pauline diverted a potentially tricky situation by suggesting, 'You can show

Harry how good you are at bowling.'

'I'm batting first,' Harry said, snatching up the stumps and the makeshift wicket that Russ had cobbled together with bits of spare wood. 'Come on.' He sped off across the sand with Mikey in hot pursuit.

'Not too far,' Pauline called after them. 'Don't go out of sight.'

Neither boy acknowledged her call. With a sigh she set about tidying up the rubbish and repacking the basket.

★ ★ ★

Angela rubbed her eyes. Close computer work made them ache but her thesis was finished. She would print it out later and check it through and make any last-minute corrections once she'd read a hard copy. Right now she was in need of a long cool drink.

The ringing of the telephone interrupted her search for ice in the cold box. It stopped before she could get to it but moments later it started up again.

With a sigh she again abandoned her search for ice, put down her drink and padded up the hall.

'Hello?' she said as she picked up the receiver.

'Angela?' Her heart sank at the voice down the other end of the line. 'Russ here.'

Ever since her talk with her mother when Isobel had voiced her concern about their relationship and the effect it might have on her career, and after what Jack had said, Angela hadn't been sure what she would say to Russ should he get in touch.

'How are things?' She kept her voice friendly, but not too friendly. 'I've been in the garden working on my thesis.'

'Ma isn't with you is she?' Russ didn't answer her question.

'No.'

'Is Isobel there?'

'She's out.'

'You don't think she and Ma have gone somewhere?'

'It's my mother's delivery day. Pauline would hardly accompany her on her rounds. What's this all about, Russ?'

'I know I shouldn't ask,' Russ began, then lapsed into silence.

'Is something wrong?'

'I can't raise Ma on the telephone at Jacob's Bluff.'

Angela relaxed.

'Is that all? She's probably enjoying the sunshine.'

'It's gone four o'clock.'

'It's not that late.'

'Harry was going to spend the day with Mikey. There was some talk about a picnic. They should be back by now.'

'Have you tried her mobile?'

'The signal's poor and she's not answering.'

'I shouldn't worry about it. I expect they've forgotten the time.'

'I wouldn't normally be too concerned but I've had Harry's mother on the line. He had a dental check-up at half three and he hasn't turned up. Like me, Mrs

Wilkes couldn't get hold of Ma.'

'Did Pauline know about this dental appointment?'

'Yes and it's not the sort of thing she'd forget.'

'Do you think the car's broken down?' Angela asked.

'I thought of that and I telephoned Jack but he's out too. He's not with you is he?'

'No one's with me. I told you I'm on my own. What do you want me to do?' Angela asked, biting down her irritation. Why did the Strettons always come crashing back into her life?

'I thought if you weren't busy,' Russ rushed on, not giving her a chance to interrupt. 'I mean I know you've always got masses to do, but could you check out Jacob's Bluff?'

'Now?'

'I'd be really grateful.'

'I'll have to cycle up.'

'Fine.'

'OK, leave it with me.' Angela abandoned all idea of sitting in the garden for what remained of the afternoon.

'If no one's there will you call me immediately?'

'Where are you?'

'Newmarket. I would come home but I don't want to go haring off on a wild goose chase.'

'I'm sure everything's fine.' Angela did her best to calm Russ down knowing it wouldn't do any good for her to draw his attention to the fact that she might be the one going off on a wild goose chase.

'Ma's hip has been playing up. I only hope she hasn't fallen.'

'Leave it with me.' Angela ended the call.

A bike ride would clear her head she decided. It was a lovely afternoon and it seemed a shame to waste it indoors. Scribbling a note for Isobel and leaving it on the kitchen table, she wheeled her bicycle out of the shed.

It had been several weeks since she had ridden the route to Jacob's Bluff and the wayside verges were now verdant and bursting with life. A scent of budding lavender drifted across the air. Soon the fields would be in full bloom ready for the summer visitors. Angela loved to see the purple flowers in their straight rows, swaying in the breeze, straight as soldiers.

Her calves ached as she increased the pressure on the pedals as she rounded the point and began the ascent towards the house. Ten minutes later, breathing heavily, she freewheeled round to the back entrance and retrieving her mother's set of keys from her basket opened the kitchen door.

'Pauline?' she called out. 'Are you there? It's Angela.'

The boiler hummed and there was a rhythmic throb from the fridge but the house echoed to the sound of her voice.

'Anybody in?' Angela went into the hall. Again her greeting was met with silence.

She glanced at her wristwatch. It was

now nearly five o'clock, way past the time for Harry's trip to the dentist. It was also getting on the late side for Pauline to be out with Mikey. She felt her first serious twinge of concern.

With one foot on the bottom step Angela was about to mount the staircase when the telephone burst into life.

'Pauline, is that you?' She snatched it up.

'Help,' a faint voice called down the line, 'help.'

'Who is this?' Angela shouted as the voice began to fade.

There was another muffled sob before the word 'help' was repeated.

'Mikey?' There was something about the voice that was familiar. 'Is that you?'

'It's Grandma.'

'Where are you?'

'We were playing cricket. Grandma fell asleep. The tide came in and we're trapped.'

In the background she could hear

Harry's urgent shouting.

'Grandma's fallen down. She's ever so pale and she's moaning. I don't know what to do.'

The line went dead.

14

Angela stabbed the recall button so hard it jarred her finger. A recorded message advised the call could not be connected. Heaving sobs rose in her chest as she tried again.

The buzzing in her ears blurred the operator's voice as she enquired, 'Emergency. Which service please?'

'Ambulance,' she gasped, 'two boys and an elderly lady are in trouble.'

'What sort of trouble?' the calm voice enquired.

'The lady is injured and the tide is coming in. Please do something. They're stranded on the beach north of Jacob's Bluff.'

'And you are?'

'Angela Banks.' She raised her voice as loud as she dared. 'My name isn't important. Please hurry.'

A shadow fell across the hall.

'Whatever's wrong?' Isobel stood in the doorway. 'Why are you shouting? Has there been an accident?'

Angela almost fell into her mother's arms.

'Did you drive up here?'

'Yes. I came to collect my picnic basket.'

'Where's your car?'

'Outside. Angela, wait.'

Angela grabbed the keys out of her mother's hand.

'Where are you going?' There was rising concern in Isobel's voice now.

'Telephone Russ. Tell him I'm on my way to the north bay.'

'Where is he?' Isobel called after her but Angela had already started the car.

Unaccustomed to the manual gear change after Pauline's automatic, Angela's foot slipped off the clutch and the car catapulted forward with a lurch, narrowly missing one of the stone statues lining the driveway. She swung the steering wheel counter-clockwise. Gravel spattered in all directions as she roared out of the gates.

A startled pheasant screeched and scuttled back into the bracken, its tail feathers switching against the paintwork. Angela put her foot down ignoring the tight bands of pressure constricting her chest.

Road signs sped past as she increased her speed. The wail of a siren behind her grew louder and she caught the reflection of a blue light flashing in her wing mirror. A police car overtook and signalled her to pull over.

She wound down the window. 'North bay? Do you know it?' she gasped at the approaching police officer.

'Good afternoon, madam,' he responded. 'May I see your driving licence?'

'What for?' Angela gulped.

'Do you know what speed you were doing?'

'You don't understand. This is an emergency.'

'Your driving licence, please,' he repeated his request in an official voice.

'I don't know where it is.'

'Do you have any means of identification?'

'Please, we're wasting time.'

'May I have your name?'

'Angela Banks.'

'Do you know the speed limit along this stretch of road, Miss Banks?'

'I wasn't speeding,' she insisted, 'I was trying to get to the north bay. There's been an accident and two young boys are stranded on the beach.'

'Can you tell me the registration number of your car?'

'What? No.'

'Is this your car, madam?'

'No, it isn't.'

'Then would you mind stepping out please?'

'There isn't time,' she insisted.

'If you wouldn't mind, madam.' His face was impassive as he held open the driver's door, his body language indicating that further protest would be pointless.

'I borrowed the car off my mother,'

she attempted to explain. 'Her name is Isobel Banks. You can check with her.'

A second police officer leaned out of the passenger door of the patrol car as the first policeman began inspecting the tyre treads.

'Emergency, Dave,' he called out, 'incident involving two children and an elderly lady. A Miss Banks has rung through.'

'That's what I've been trying to tell you.' Angela clutched the police officer's sleeve. 'The injured lady is Mrs Pauline Stretton and I got a call from Mikey saying the tide was coming in. They're stranded and Mrs Stretton is injured.'

'Mikey?'

'Her grandson. He's only five years old. You have to let me through.' Angela's voice gave out on her.

'Where did you say this was?' The tone of the policeman's voice changed.

'The bay north of Jacob's Bluff. I'll show you the way.'

'Go on ahead then, but keep to the

speed limit,' the policeman warned, 'we don't want any more accidents.'

Angela's whole body was shaking as she sank back into the driving seat. Dark clouds scudded across the sky and a fat blob of rain landed on the windscreen. It was swiftly followed by several more, obliterating her vision. In the background she could hear static police announcements over the radio as she tried to activate her wipers. Blurred blue lights flashed relentlessly through the smeared windscreen.

An ambulance raced past and more sirens began to wail as the police car abandoned its wait for her to start up and took off after the ambulance.

There was a loud swish as the wipers cleared her windscreen and Angela eased back onto the road. All the lights were against her and cars that had pulled over to let the emergency vehicles through now drew out in front of her. Angela wanted to scream at them to get out of the way. Every second was precious.

Eventually she swung off the main road and splashed through the muddy potholed lane leading down towards the sand dunes. Isobel's exhaust protested at the harsh treatment. Angela prayed it would stay the course.

Through her open window she could hear radio noises, and flashing lights were arcing the evening sky. She caught a flash of high-visibility jackets as two paramedics unloaded a rolling stretcher from a parked ambulance.

'It's this way.' She gestured with her arms and deserting her car, began running, her feet slipping in the sand. Down in the bay two small figures were huddled together on a rock that was encircled by the rising water.

'Mikey? Harry?' she yelled at the boys. 'I'm coming down.'

'Steady how you go,' one of the paramedics panted after her, 'watch out for the undercurrent.'

Ignoring the warning Angela splashed through the rising water. It swirled round her legs, dragging her down.

'Stay where you are,' she screeched at Mikey. Harry had already jumped off the rock.

'We put the picnic rung over Mrs Stretton to keep her warm,' he shouted. 'I'll show you where she is.'

'It's alright, son,' one of police officers said as he reached Mikey. 'We're here now.'

'I'm his teacher,' Angela said, pushing him to one side, 'and a friend of the family. Let me see to him.'

'Take him up to the ambulance,' a paramedic instructed her. 'Now where's the patient?' He waded across to Harry, who was clinging to a small circle of rocks that allowed some protection from the rising tide.

'We climbed on the rock to wait for you, then we couldn't get off,' Mikey stammered, his teeth chattering.

Angela held out her hand and gave him a bright smile, anxious not to alarm him further. 'We need to help each other back up to the dunes.'

'I wasn't frightened,' Mikey insisted,

clasping her hand and looking at her with eyes that were over-bright.

'I know that and you can tell me all about it when we're on dry land.'

'What's that?' Mikey pointed to a black dot circling in the sky above them. 'It's getting bigger.'

The whine of rotor blades grew louder.

'It's a helicopter.' Angela's voice was almost drowned out by the noise.

'Is it for Grandma?' Mikey's brown eyes were wide with wonder. 'Is she safe now?'

'She's fine but I expect they'll want to transport her to hospital to carry out checks.' Angela tugged at his arm. 'Let's get out of their way.'

Together they splashed through the swirling water, Angela keeping firm hold of her charge who now showed signs of wanting to linger to catch all the action.

'Grandma was trying to keep up with us,' he panted as Angela dragged him along. 'We were hurrying up the beach with all our stuff. Then she fell. Harry said he didn't mind if Grandma wanted to lean on his shoulder and we got her to the rocks. Then Harry put the rug over Grandma, to keep her warm, but it was covered in crisps and bits of banana and I don't think she would like that. We searched for her telephone and she told me to press the first button and you answered,' he finished in a rush.

'You've been a very brave boy,' Angela soothed.

'Harry was brave too,' Mikey volunteered.

'You both were. Now let's get you to the ambulance.'

'What about Harry?' Mikey looked over his shoulder. 'We can't leave him.'

'We're right behind you,' a police officer said as he waded towards them. 'Off you go, son, with your teacher. We'll deal with this.'

'I want to help,' Harry insisted.

'You have been a great help already but the best thing you can do now is to go with Miss Banks and Mikey. We'll tell you all about it later.'

'Promise?'

The rain was setting up a steady drizzle and by the time the bedraggled trio reached the ambulance their clothes were soaked through.

'I was s'posed to go the dentist,' Harry chattered through shivering teeth.

'Someone will call your mother for you,' Angela explained. 'Let's get you warmed up first.'

'This is exciting,' Harry enthused. Already he was looking less pale and some of the colour was coming back to Mikey's face.

Angela was pleased to see how his presence had a calming effect on Mikey as the two boys vied for position of top dog.

'I noticed the tide was coming in,' Harry boasted.

'I woke Grandma from her nap,' Mikey retaliated.

'You were both brilliant.' The female paramedic guided them up the steps of the ambulance. 'Let's get you lads sorted out. You're very wet and we don't want anyone catching a cold.'

'This is our teacher,' Harry explained, 'it's half term and we went on a picnic with Mikey's grandma.'

'What an exciting time you've had. Now come along, first things first.'

Angela did her best to shield the boys from Pauline's air rescue as the sound of the helicopter hovering overhead was making conversation difficult.

'Can we draw this for our half term holiday picture, Miss?' Harry asked after the medic had carried out a quick check on the boys to make sure there was no risk of hypothermia.

'Let's wait and see.' Angela rubbed his wet hair with a towel in the back of the ambulance.

It was warm inside the vehicle and with hot drinks inside them the boys began to revive. To Angela's relief they appeared to have suffered no ill effects from their experience and they were soon dry and as comfortable as the conditions allowed.

'What about you?' the paramedic asked Angela as the boys munched on emergency rations of chocolate.

Until now Angela hadn't noticed her dress was soaked and clinging to her back. She peeled off her cardigan.

'Give it here. What about your dress?'

'I've got no intention of undressing in the back of an ambulance,' she insisted, 'especially not with two of my pupils looking on.'

The paramedic gave her a sympathetic grin.

'Put this round you then.' She produced a blanket.

'You do look funny,' Harry giggled, 'like an Indian chief sitting outside a wigwam. You only need feathers in your hair.'

'You should remember your manners, young man,' the paramedic reprimanded him, 'and share some of that chocolate with Miss Banks. She's had a shock too you know.'

The din from the helicopter grew fainter and a few moments later a policeman poked his head through the rear door of the ambulance.

'Miss Banks? A word?' He indicated that she should step to one side to avoid being overheard.

'How is Mrs Stretton?' she asked, her mask of confidence slipping now the boys could no longer see her.

'She's been airlifted to hospital.'

'The boys only gave me a garbled version of what happened.'

'As far as we can make out the tide cut them off. They were making for safety when Mrs Stretton fell. Young Harry showed great presence of mind helping and covered her in the picnic rug. They took refuge on a rock because they didn't want to leave her, then the sea swept in.'

Angela closed her eyes. The consequences didn't bear thinking about.

'I understand the lady's hip was troubling her?' the policeman asked.

'Yes. She has been experiencing some pain,' Angela replied.

'Do you know her next of kin?'

'Her son, Russ. He was worried when he couldn't raise Mrs Stretton on the telephone and that's why I was up at the house. He asked me to check on her. He doesn't know what's happened.'

'Don't worry. We'll get in touch with him and young Harry's mother. He gave us the number. Now for the moment we're all finished here. What's happening to the boys?'

'What they really need is a hot bath, then bed. I'll take them back to Jacob's Bluff. That's where Mrs Stretton lives.'

'Drive carefully then and remember to observe the speed limit.'

'Just going to fetch the car.' Angela poked her head back into the ambulance.

'Not dressed like that you're not,' the paramedic said. 'Here, you'd better wear this.' She produced a high-visibility jacket that came to Angela's knees. 'Not the height of fashion but it will have to do,' she added as Angela wriggled out of her blanket and shrugged it on.

'Won't be too long then we'll be off,' she said to Harry and Mikey, who had been giggling at her attempts to maintain her modesty.

Back at the car she retrieved her mobile from the passenger seat. There were five missed calls and they were all from Russ.

15

Angela drew up outside Jacob's Bluff. The house was a blaze of light. Exhausted by events the boys had fallen asleep in the back seat of the car, only stirring when Angela let in a cold blast of air as she opened the driver's door.

'Darling.' Harry's mother flew down the steps, arms outstretched, and yanked open the rear door.

'Mum, it was brilliant.' Refreshed by his forty winks, Harry was now fully awake but barely had time to speak before Mrs Wilkes scooped him up in her arms.

'I've been so worried about you.'

Harry wriggled free from her embrace anxious to get on with his story.

'Mikey and I were playing cricket. Before that we were searching for buried treasure in the sand,' he began to recount his adventure.

'You can tell me later.' She smoothed back his hair in a gesture of maternal concern then satisfied that her son was no worse the wear for the experience, thanked Angela for bringing her son safely home.

'They've had a medical check-up in the ambulance,' Angela explained, 'but neither of the boys appeared to have suffered any ill effects, although maybe I would suggest a couple of quiet days?'

'I should be so lucky.' Mrs Wilkes raised her eyes. 'I'd better get this one off home. He's practically dead on his feet. His brothers were so jealous when they heard what happened, I doubt whether I'll get any of them to sleep tonight.'

Angela was grateful that Mrs Wilkes was not the sort to make a fuss.

'Bye, Mikey. Bye, Miss Banks.'

Still chattering excitedly, Harry allowed his mother to hold his hand as they made their way to her car.

'Papa.' Mikey skipped up and down, now anxious to be the centre of attention. 'There was a helicopter and the police and an ambulance. We ate chocolate in the ambulance and drank hot milk, yuk,' he made a face as he remembered he didn't like hot milk, 'and the promedic lady asked us if we were cold and put some funny silver stuff over us.'

'He means paramedic,' Angela explained gently, restraining Mikey's exuberance.

As Russ's eyes took in her appearance she remembered she was still wearing the highly unflattering high-visibility jacket the paramedic had provided.

'I'm glad my son doesn't seem to have suffered unduly from the trauma.' Russ kept his voice low. 'How about you? And what happened to your clothes?'

'My dress was soaked but I'm fine.'

'Of course she's fine.' Isobel had been hovering behind Russ. 'I brought my daughter up to deal with life's little emergencies. Now, would you like me to look after Mikey while you have a

226

private word with Angela? I'm sure you've lots to discuss. I fear your son is in danger of getting over-excited and if we carry on like this there'll be tears before bedtime.'

'But I want to tell Papa everything that happened,' Mikey protested.

'Come along, Mikey.' Isobel held out her hand. 'I want to hear what you've been up to. You can tell Papa later.'

Alone on the steps outside Jacob's Bluff, Angela began to feel extremely self-conscious in her unconventional garb and uncomfortably warm.

'Your mother's made coffee and sandwiches for us in the kitchen,' Russ informed her.

Now the excitement was over other emotions were kicking in. Angela felt flat as if someone had burst her party balloon. She trailed down the hall behind Russ. The harsh glare from the overhead strip lighting in the kitchen stung the back of her eyes after the gloom outside.

'I'll turn them down.' Russ noticed

her wince and adjusted the strength. 'That better?'

'Thank you.'

She wrinkled her nose as she sniffed her fingers. 'I smell of seaweed.'

'You can have a shower if you like,' Russ offered, 'there's masses of hot water.'

'I'll just wash my hands and face,' Angela insisted. 'If I have a shower I'm in serious danger of falling asleep afterwards.'

'You know where the facilities are. I'll heat up the coffee unless you would prefer anything stronger?'

'Coffee will be fine,' Angela assured him, going into the small pantry at the side of the kitchen.

She ran some water over her face and tried to repair the damage to her hair, with a quick comb through. Finding a flowered overall belonging to her mother hanging on a hook on the back of the door, she changed out of the high-visibility jacket and put it on. She immediately felt more comfortable.

Russ was seated at the table and looked ready to attack the plate of sandwiches.

'Better?'

'Much,' she replied and sat down opposite him.

'We've got cheese and tomato, cold beef with mustard and egg and cress, a feast fit for a king. Tuck in.'

Angela was surprised to discover how hungry she was. As well as the sandwiches Isobel had produced one of her special farmhouse fruitcakes, and after two mugs of hot coffee Angela began to feel more like her old self.

'I got your voice mail messages,' she said. 'I had asked my mother to call you,' she explained as she refused more coffee, 'before I realised she didn't know where you were.'

'It doesn't matter,' Russ insisted. 'Everyone's safe. That's the most important thing. I know it sounds inadequate, but thank you. I should never have asked you to do what you did.'

Angela's cheeks flamed from the intensity of his eyes fixed on hers.

'You might not have been quite so grateful if you'd seen how I behaved when the police stopped me for speeding. If the emergency call hadn't come through when it did I'd probably have been on the front page of the local paper charged with assault and battery. No one was listening to me.'

'Then I'm glad they finally did.'

Russ's voice sounded deeper in the confines of the kitchen. The caffeine kicked in and Angela wondered if she would ever get to sleep that night. With her senses heightened, her fingertips tingled and her circulation began to return to normal as Russ recounted his story. He had, it appeared, learned most of what happened from the police.

'They tracked down Harry's mother and she gave them my number. I got back just as Mrs Wilkes arrived. We found Isobel pacing up and down outside not knowing what was going on. We could hear the emergency helicopter circling overhead but as you'd made off with your mother's car Isobel was stranded and totally in the dark as to developments. Everyone took some calming down I can tell you.'

'Harry seems to think it was all put on for his entertainment.' Angela's generous mouth curved into a wide smile as relief relaxed her concern over what had happened.

'Am I glad Mrs Wilkes doesn't do hissy fits,' Russ admitted. 'I don't think I could have coped.'

'Then it's just as well I'm not about to have one either.' Angela sagged against the back of her chair. 'I don't think I've got the energy.'

Russ leaned across the table and imprisoned her wrist under his fingers.

'Angela. There's something I want to say to you.'

'Has anyone informed Judith about all this?' Angela yanked her hand out of his grasp, a gesture not lost on Russ. 'I dread to think of the mileage she'll make out of it.'

'She can't blame you for what happened.'

'She'll have a good try.'

'I doubt whether my mother's in any position to offer a detailed explanation so for the moment it might be better if Judith remained in the dark.'

'Shouldn't you be at the hospital?' Angela asked, determined to keep the conversation away from personal emotions.

'The nurse in charge has assured me she is comfortable. For the moment there's nothing much else I can do. I can't leave Mikey alone. I'll call again in the morning after the doctors have done their rounds.'

Russ's eyes were still fixed on Angela with an intensity that was making her uncomfortable.

'If she wasn't so stubborn,' he continued, 'this hip business would have been sorted out ages ago but she's the last person in this world to admit to weakness. It's a generation thing. She was raised to put up and shut up.'

There was a thud from upstairs and the sound of movement in the bathroom.

'I should be going,' Angela said.

'You can't leave without Isobel and it sounds as though she's busy, so you're stuck with my company for the time being, unappealing as the prospect is.'

Angela flinched. She wanted to justify her reaction to Russ's touch but the present mood was wrong for that type of in-depth discussion and she didn't know how to explain why she couldn't get involved with him.

'Judith,' she began.

'Do we have to talk about Judith?'

'Yes we do. Don't you realise we have handed her the perfect excuse to return to Paris with Mikey? She'll insist you've lost the plot and I'm a bad influence on you, or something like that.'

A shuttered look came over Russ's face.

'Things will have to wait until I've got a clearer head on me,' he replied, 'but I can allay your fears. As yet no decision has been made regarding Mikey's future and I'd be grateful if you didn't mention anything to him.'

'Of course I won't.'

A gentle tap interrupted them.

Isobel poked her head round the kitchen door. 'Mikey's almost asleep, Russ, but he wants you to go up and say good night. I don't think he'll settle until he sees you.'

'In that case I'd better do as my son commands. Can you see yourselves out?'

'We know the way,' Isobel replied. 'Let us know if there's anything you'd like us to do won't you?' she offered.

'I won't trouble you any more. Thank you, Isobel.'

Isobel raised her eyebrows at her daughter after Russ's abrupt departure from the kitchen.

'Have you had words?' she whispered.

'I was bearing your advice in mind.' Angela began gathering up her things. 'I didn't think letting Russ hold my hand across the kitchen table would have gone down well with the board of governors, should they ever find out about it, and there are enough spies about the place to tell tales.' Angela's voice threatened to give out on her.

'You're tired. Come on, let's get you home,' Isobel sympathised, 'we've had more than enough emotion for one day.'

'Give me a noisy classroom any time,' Angela agreed.

At the end of her first day back at school after the half term break Angela was beginning to regret those words. Several of the children had been unwell and sent home after the doctor was called and diagnosed a bug doing the rounds. There had been an accident in the playground and while she had been tending to a scraped knee a serious squabble had broken out between two of the more aggressive boys, resulting in Angela receiving a nasty bruised ankle as she tried to separate them. By the end of the afternoon she was hobbling around the classroom, her head was aching and she was beginning to wish she hadn't applied for the job of head teacher.

'My goodness, what have you done to your foot?' Harry's mother greeted her at the school gate after the last bell of the day had rung. 'Nothing to do with recent events was it?'

'Nothing at all,' Angela reassured her, trying to make light of the incident.

'My Harry hasn't stopped talking about helicopters and emergency vehicles. His brothers are so envious.'

'Mikey seems none the worse for the experience,' Angela replied.

Like Harry he had returned to school that morning and both of them could be heard in the playground regaling their classmates of all the details of their adventure.

'You're looking stressed. Remember to take some time out for yourself,' Mrs Wilkes advised. 'I find it's the only way to get through.'

Thanking her for her concern, Angela

made to leave but was detained by Mrs Wilkes clutching at her sleeve.

'I think that young man is trying to attract your attention.' She nodded across the playground. 'Jack, isn't it?'

'Hi, Angela. I'm doing Mikey's school run,' Jack Brewer greeted her. 'It's all been OK'd with Russ and Judith.'

'Judith's back?'

'Didn't you know? Where's my charge?'

'He's still in the cloakroom.'

'Time for a few quiet words then. Have you given any more thought to our dinner date?' Jack asked. 'I'm free this evening and from what I've been hearing you could do with a night out. No strings attached?'

Angela looked down at her bruised ankle. What she wanted was a hot bath and an early night.

'Another time?'

'You're a hard girl to pin down.' Jack looked disappointed. 'Don't head teachers get any time off?'

'I'm not there yet,' Angela replied.

'It's in the bag. How about Wednesday? There, that's plenty of advance warning.'

'Wednesday would be fine,' Angela agreed, unable to think of any more excuses to turn him down.

'Come on then, Mikey,' Jack greeted his young charge who had come tearing out of the cloakroom to greet him. 'Let's get you home.'

'Have you heard about my adventure, Uncle Jack?' he demanded. 'We had the helicopter and the police.' His voice trailed away as the two of them made their way to Jack's car.

Mrs Potter had left early, as her daughter had been one of those affected with the bug and now she was alone, Angela did a final read-through of her thesis, which she intended to hand over in the morning. She signed off the last page as the telephone rang on the desk.

'St Andrew's,' she said as she picked up the receiver.

'You're still there?'

'Russ, what can I do for you?'

'Did Jack pick up Mikey?'

'About half past three. Are you checking up on him?'

'I wanted to make sure, that's all.'

'There's no need to worry. It went like clockwork.'

'I'm glad something did.' There was a pause. 'Judith's back. Did you know?'

'Jack mentioned it. How's Pauline?' she asked.

'Getting under everyone's skin at the hospital. Still, it's a great help having Judith here. She's proving surprisingly helpful in the house answering the phone and taking messages, that sort of thing.'

'Fine. Was there anything else?' Angela looked to finish the call.

'I was wondering if you'd like to go out to dinner on Wednesday night, as a thank-you? I'd like to make amends for being so abrupt last week. It was bordering on rude. I'm sorry.'

Angela paused before saying, 'I can't do Wednesday.'

'Is that a diplomatic 'can't do' or are you really double-booked?'

Angela bridled at the scepticism in Russ's voice. 'If you must know I'm going out to dinner with Jack,' she replied. 'Now if you'll excuse me I have my thesis to finish.'

16

'Congratulations.' Jack raised his glass. 'I told you it wasn't in doubt didn't I?'

'Thank you.' Angela chinked her glass against his. 'And yes you did,' she admitted.

'When did you get the news?'

'After the children had gone home.'

'So it's hot off the press?'

'I've only told my mother and you,' Angela admitted.

'St Andrew's junior wing will be in very capable hands. What shall we have to celebrate your new promotion? You're a girl who knows her own mind but I can recommend the Frutti di Mare — that's seafood for those whose Italian is a bit rusty.'

'You've entertained female friends here before?' Angela peered at Jack over the top of her menu.

'I haven't.' Jack did his best to look

hurt at the assumption. 'Two of my mechanics recommended the place. Said it was the best seafood risotto they'd ever had.'

'Seafood risotto it is then.'

After Jack had ordered, Angela sipped her wine. Her head was still in a whirl. She hadn't expected to receive the news of her appointment so soon after submitting her thesis.

'I won't have to call you Miss Banks from now on will I?' Jack joked.

'Only in front of the children.'

'I'll do my best to remember,' he promised solemnly. 'By the way can I go public on this? Some of the lads have been asking me about you. It seems everyone knows someone at St Andrew's. It's got a good reputation.'

'Which I intend to uphold and yes, you can go public.'

Jack's enthusiasm was infectious and Angela was pleased she had accepted his invitation to dinner. The bruise on her leg was less swollen now and after a good night's sleep she had been back to her old self the next day.

'I think we are dining at the latest in place.' Jack looked round. The atmosphere in the restaurant was vibrant and nearly all the tables were full. 'I had to promise a discount on the manager's next five-thousand-miles' service to get a booking,' Jack admitted. 'Wednesday is a popular night.'

Angela smiled at the proprietor as he checked with them that everything was to their satisfaction.

'My granddaughter would never speak to me again if I told her that her beloved teacher Miss Banks had not been happy with her meal.' He kissed his fingers at her. 'Enjoy.'

'I didn't realise you were such a local celebrity,' Jack said.

Angela acknowledged more smiles from fellow diners. 'I'll have to be on my best behaviour.'

'And I was so looking forward to dancing on the table.' Jack's face was deadpan. 'Another time perhaps?'

'There'll be none of that, now or

later,' Angela responded.

'Yes, miss.' Jack pulled a face, then added, 'Spoilsport.'

'To change the subject,' Angela asked carefully, 'have you seen Judith?'

Jack's mouth twisted into a rueful smile.

'I have,' he admitted then paused. Angela said nothing, waiting for him to go on. 'She's not a very happy bunny.'

'I can imagine,' Angela admitted. 'I was expecting to get the blame for what happened on the north beach so I have stayed out of her way. With you doing Mikey's school run it hasn't been a problem. Now she's a lady of means I suppose there'll be no stopping her.'

'You haven't heard?' Jack queried.

'Heard what?'

'I thought Isobel might have told you. She's up at the house most days.'

'You know my mother doesn't gossip.'

'She's the most discreet person I know.' Jack smiled. 'I suspect she knows most of what goes on round here but she never repeats anything. You don't think she could be tempted to divulge the down and dirty on my mechanics? I'm sure they get up to all sorts of goings on when my back is turned.'

'No she wouldn't. And what were you saying,' Angela prompted, 'about Judith?'

Jack's eyes danced with laughter.

'You've got to promise to keep a straight face.'

'All right.' Intrigued, Angela urged him, 'Go on.'

'That inheritance you were referring to? The one Judith raced back to France to cash in on? We all thought she'd come into a fortune from an uncle who owned a château?'

'There's no inheritance?'

'There's an inheritance all right but not quite what she was expecting.'

'What do you mean?'

'It seems the uncle left her a tumble-down old well.'

'What?' Angela strung the word out in disbelief.

'It's a horrible thing apparently. It's

been boarded up for years and it's stuck away in a deserted part of the grounds of this big château.'

'Who inherits the château?'

'No one. Judith thought her uncle owned it but he didn't.'

'Only the well?'

'Got it in one. He won it apparently many years ago in a game of cards, so the story goes. By all accounts he had led a colourful life.'

'So Judith isn't going to be lady of the manor?'

''Fraid not. She was not best pleased. I suppose you don't know anyone who would be interested in buying an old French water well?'

They both burst out laughing, their amusement earning them surprised glances from the other diners.

'You broke your promise,' Jack accused Angela when he recovered himself. 'You said you'd keep a straight face.'

'I'm really sorry but that's the funniest thing I've heard in years.'

'Judith didn't see the funny side of it.'

'What's she going to do now?'

'I have no idea. I haven't actually seen much of her. With Pauline Stretton still in hospital and Russ always on the move her time had been taken up looking after Mikey and running the house. I've been doing the school run for her but we've really only exchanged a few words.'

'You haven't seen her socially?'

'Would you mind if I had?' Jack looked unnaturally serious.

'Not in the least.' Angela refused to rise to his bait.

'May I know why?'

'You know our relationship is that of old friends,' Angela answered.

'Even though I'd like it to be more?'

'It could never be that,' Angela was adamant.

'It's Russ, isn't it?' Jack asked quietly.

'What's Russ?' Angela demanded.

'You held off from getting involved with him because he is the father of one of your pupils and you were in line for this head teacher appointment.' Jack held up a hand to stop her from interrupting. 'It was the only sensible course of action. Anyone else would have done the same.'

'It wasn't quite like that.'

'This is Jack you're talking to,' he coaxed as Angela struggled to find the right words.

'Now Judith's back it doesn't matter how I feel about Russ,' Angela replied, 'they're an item.'

'Not any more they're not,' Jack replied.

'Not officially, but from what you've told me, she's not going to rush Mikey back to France now is she?'

'I think there's something you should know about Judith and her plans to return to France,' Jack spoke slowly and carefully, 'although it's nothing concrete.' He hesitated as if uncertain how to continue.

'But?' Angela prompted.

'If my suspicions are correct she plans to fly to France in the not-too-distant future and I also suspect she'll leave after dark.'

'With Mikey?'

'Yes.'

'Why after dark?'

'No one will see her.'

'So Pauline was right.'

'What do you mean?' Jack demanded.

'She said Judith would make it worth your while. That's why you were driving her around the countryside. Dry run was it? For the big day, or should I say night?'

'It wasn't like that,' Jack tried to explain.

'Norwich of course.' Angela smacked her brow with the palm of her hand. 'It's making sense to me now.'

'Not to me it isn't,' Jack grumbled.

'She's going to fly from Norwich isn't she?'

'I keep telling you we didn't go to Norwich.'

'But you did visit the airport?'

'Only to have a look,' Jack insisted.

'Didn't you suspect anything?' Angela demanded.

'Why would I?'

Angela raised her eyes.

'Honestly, Jack, sometimes I despair of you, but never mind about that. We have to tell Russ.'

'All in good time.'

'Now,' Angela insisted.

'Look, best not get involved.'

'We can't ignore our suspicions.'

'We can. It's none of our business.'

'I disagree.'

'I'm beginning to wish I'd never told you.'

'I'm glad you did.'

Angela pushed back her chair.

'Where are you going?' Jack looked up in alarm.

'Thank you for dinner.'

'Don't you want any dessert? Why the rush?'

'Judith may act tonight.'

'That's highly unlikely.'

'We can't take the risk.'

'If you're intent on going up to Jacob's Bluff then I'm coming with you.'

'I can go on my own.'

'How do you intend getting up there?' Jack threw some notes down onto the table. 'On your bicycle?'

Angela bit her lip in vexation.

'Why didn't you tell me what you suspected Judith was up to before now?'

'I might have done but you turned down my first dinner invitation, remember? Something about cosying up to a mug of cocoa?'

Angela shrugged on her coat. 'Hurry up,' she implored. 'There's no time to lose.'

'Miss Banks?' The proprietor rushed over. 'Is something is wrong?'

'Everything was fine,' Jack assured him.

'Thank you,' Angela called over her shoulder.

'Bit of an emergency has come up. Sorry,' Jack apologised. 'This should cover the bill.' He thrust the notes at the proprietor. 'Bring your car in next week. I'll personally see to its service. Lovely meal.'

He rushed out in hot pursuit of Angela, who was pacing up and down the pavement.

'Where's your car?'

The only vehicle parked outside the restaurant was a gleaming red Italian sports car.

'Right here. I'm test driving it.' Jack opened the door. 'Jump in. Let's see how it reacts in an emergency.'

The car surged forward with a powerful thrust. The night was warm and several strolling pedestrians turned at the sound of the throaty roar as Jack eased the car down the main street before turning off towards the road that led to Jacob's Bluff.

'We shouldn't be getting involved,' he repeated as they sped along.

'Don't you dare turn back now, Jack Brewer.' Angela glared across at him.

Jack gave an exaggerated sigh. 'If only I'd had the sense to keep quiet.'

Angela clenched her fists. 'I can't believe you didn't mention it earlier.'

'At the risk of repeating myself it was

none of my business.'

'Are you absolutely sure Judith wants to leave after dark?'

'It's only guesswork on my part but if she were to leave during the day someone would notice.'

'What alerted you to her plans in the first place?'

'I caught her chatting up one of my mechanics. It seemed a bit odd because it sounded as though she was making a date with him. That's when my suspicions became aroused. He's married with a young family and always short of cash. When I saw her pass some money over I wondered why. It was only when I thought about it later I put two and two together.'

'Why didn't she ask you to be her driver?'

'I suspect it was because she couldn't be sure I wouldn't tell you or Russ. I would have turned her down anyway. I am actually quite honourable,' Jack insisted.

'I feel so sorry for Mikey.'

'Children are resilient. He'll think it's another great adventure. I shouldn't worry too much.'

'What makes you such an expert on child psychology?'

'Now, now, Miss Banks,' Jack chided, 'don't go all tetchy on me. I'm the hero of the hour. Remember?'

'Only if we get to Jacob's Bluff in time.'

As she spoke Jack was forced to brake suddenly to avoid going into the back of a farm tractor that had pulled out in front of them. He hooted loudly, earning a shaken fist from the driver, who continued to trundle along in front of them.

'Do something,' Angela insisted.

'Like what? I've tried hooting and all I got was a rather rude hand gesture. I'm not going to try any clever overtaking in this car, it's not mine, remember? We are going to have to sit it out, and mind the upholstery. We don't want any scratch marks from where your nails have dug in the leatherwork.'

'He's turning off.' Angela grabbed Jack's arm.

'Steady. This driver's not too fussy where he sprays his clods of mud and I don't think he likes us. Right.' Jack put his foot down as the tractor finished its turning manoeuvre. 'We are in a go situation. Won't be long now. Er, what exactly do you intend doing when we get to the house?'

'Confront Judith, of course. If we're in time that is.'

'And if we're not?'

Angela slumped. The back of her throat felt tight.

'I don't know,' she admitted. 'Legally Judith is within her rights to take Mikey back to France but someone has to let Russ know what she's planning.'

'We could have just rung him you know.'

'The main telephone is in the house and if he's in the studio he doesn't always answer it.'

'Failure isn't an option is it?' Jack cast Angela a look, as if he were reading her mind. 'I'll get you there in time. Have I ever let you down?'

Angela decided now was not the moment to go into detail regarding the occasions when he had been late or not turned up at all for various casual dates.

'Hate driving in the twilight.' He negotiated another tricky turn. 'Things loom out in front of you then change shape. I hope that was a cat.' A dark shadow darted across the road in front of them.

At last Jacob's Bluff came into view. To Angela's relief she saw lights on in the main house.

'Someone's there.'

'What's the time?' Jack asked.

'Nine-thirty.'

Jack drove through the gates of Jacob's Bluff. 'Right, we're here, plan of action? Main house first or studio?'

Angela swivelled round in her seat. The studio was in darkness.

'Main house,' she decided.

Jack frowned through the windscreen. 'I think the front door is open.'

As they drew up a figure ran down the steps towards them.

'You're very late. You should have been here hours ago. We're all ready.' Judith stumbled against the driver's door and peered through the window. 'What's Angela doing here?'

'We've been out to dinner.'

'You told her, didn't you?'

Angela looked from Jack to Judith, then back to Jack again.

'I don't understand,' she said faintly. 'Jack said you paid one of his mechanics to drive you to Norwich Airport.'

Judith threw back her head and laughed.

'My dear Angela, you are extremely gullible. Jack and I are going back to France together and we're taking Mikey with us. I don't know what story he has spun you but if you had some idea about stopping us then I'm afraid you are out of luck.'

17

'You did not suspect?' Judith's French accent was pronounced and heightened the tension between the two women.

Angela stared at the crack of light emanating from the main door. She needed to focus on something that she understood, but even the crack of light was playing tricks on her. It was changing shape.

'*Maman*?' Mikey poked his head round the gap he had created by gently pulling open the door. He was warmly dressed in bright red trousers and an anorak. 'I'm tired.'

'I know it's late, *chéri*, but Jack was delayed.'

Angela turned confused hazel eyes in Jack's direction. His blue eyes challenged the expression on her face.

'You surely don't believe Judith?' He

made a gesture of appeal with his hands.

Angela felt was as if she were an actor on stage playing a part for which she was under-rehearsed.

'How could I have made plans to go away with Judith on the night we were having dinner together? It was a long-standing date,' Jack insisted.

'Long-standing?' Judith scoffed. 'I do not think so.'

'Whatever, no one's going anywhere tonight,' he insisted. 'It's too late to start driving around the countryside.'

Judith looked as though she were about to protest but was distracted by Mikey asking, 'Where's Papa?'

'Yes, where is Russ?' Angela repeated the question.

Hardly had she finished speaking when there was the sound of another vehicle approaching the gates and moments later she caught a flash of a blue and white painted logo of a private ambulance approaching the house.

'Now what?' Jack muttered under his breath.

Judith's shoulders sagged.

'You'd better all come inside. Mikey, hold my hand.'

'We're not going out?' Mikey tugged at his mother's hand and she swung him into her arms. 'That means I can go to school tomorrow? Harry and I are ball monitors.' He finished on a monster yawn. 'We've got two teams and we need a new football.' His voice faded as he leaned on his mother's shoulder. 'The old one's ever so flat.'

'Then you cannot possibly let Harry down on such an important day, can you?' There was the suspicion of a tear in Judith's eyes as she continued to smile at her son. 'How about some hot milk then bed?'

'Please,' he mumbled into her neck.

'Who's this?' Angela hissed at Jack as the ambulance drew up outside the house.

'Search me,' was the reply, 'but I'll tell you one thing, I don't think it's my mechanic come to drive Judith to the airport.'

The passenger door slid open.

'Hello, darling,' Isobel Banks greeted her daughter with a wide smile. 'Did you have a good evening?'

'What's your mother doing here?' Jack demanded in bewilderment.

'I have absolutely no idea,' Angela replied.

'Russ telephoned me,' Isobel explained, 'and said he had received a call. His mother was insisting on being discharged from hospital and would I go with him to help?'

'And naturally you agreed?' There was a note of resignation in Angela's voice.

'What else could I do?'

'Said no?' Angela suggested.

'I couldn't do that.' Isobel looked affronted by the very idea.

'What about your foot? I suppose you didn't give that a moment's thought? You were told to rest up as much as possible.'

'Nonsense, I'm fit as a flea.' Isobel brushed her daughter's concern aside. 'Besides,' she gave a light laugh, 'if we hadn't gone to collect Pauline she would have discharged herself anyway. You know how forceful she can be.' She looked around at the gathered throng on the steps of the house. 'But what are you all doing?'

'They're here to welcome me home of course, aren't they?' Pauline delivered a regal wave from the mobile stretcher one of the crew had wheeled out of the back of the ambulance.

'Grandma.' At the sound of her voice Mikey raised his head off his mother's shoulder.

Her wrinkled face broke into a smile of undiluted pleasure as he scrambled out of his mother's embrace and raced towards her.

'How's my favourite grandson? Have you missed me?'

He threw his arms round her neck. 'You're alive.'

'Very much so,' Pauline replied in a

soothing voice. 'How could you think otherwise?'

'The waves were making you wet.'

'It would take more than a bit of water to finish me off.'

Pauline's robust reply made everyone smile.

'I should have explained to Mikey that his grandmother was in hospital because of her hip,' Judith murmured half to herself, half to Angela. 'I thought he knew. My poor baby.'

'There was a lot of confusion at the time,' Angela sympathised. 'You weren't to know who had told him what.'

The beginnings of a hesitant smile softened Judith's strained face.

'That is very generous of you to think so, Angela,' she said, 'and a weight off my mind. I would hate to think my thoughtlessness would cause Mikey any further distress.'

'You should have heard Mikey and Harry regaling their classmates about what had happened. They were quite the heroes of the hour. I don't think they suffered any lasting effects.'

Judith touched Angela's arm. 'Can you forgive me?' she asked.

'Ah, the prodigal returns,' Jack interrupted as Russ stepped out of the shadows, his strained eyes moving from Judith to Angela.

'Papa,' Mikey, who had abandoned his grandmother's side, now hopped from foot to foot, '*Maman* says we're not going out tonight after all so I can stay here with you and Angela.'

'I did not put it quite like that.' Judith raised an amused eyebrow at Russ.

'Can this wait,' Pauline demanded from her prone position, 'before we all catch a chill standing around in the cold?'

'Is that your car blocking the drive?' Russ asked Jack.

Jack leapt to attention. 'I'll move it.'

'Thank you.'

'If I'm not needed any more?' He cast a querying glance at everyone. 'I'd best be on my way. It's getting late.'

'I have no need of your services,'

Russ replied. 'Judith? Angela?'

'Good night, Jack.' Judith kissed him on the cheek.

Angela contented herself with merely shaking her head.

With a look of relief and a quick wave at everyone Jack made off. The sound of his revving engine echoed down the drive as he sped off into the night.

'There goes my gallant knight in shining armour,' Judith commented with a wry twist of her lips.

'And my lift home,' Angela added.

'We'd better get you upstairs, madam,' the ambulance man addressed Pauline, 'then we can be off too.'

'Not before time,' Pauline agreed.

'I'll take Mikey shall I?' Isobel offered. 'I'm sure the three of you,' she looked at Russ, Judith and Angela, 'have things to discuss.'

'The living room in ten minutes?' The expression in Russ's eyes was unfathomable and Angela wasn't sure if he was addressing her or Judith. 'I need to freshen up.'

'An excellent idea.' Judith was the first to agree. 'Angela?' She took charge of the situation. 'This way.'

The dying embers of a coal fire smouldered in the grate. Judith shivered and closed the window.

'I shall never get used to the English weather.'

Angela knelt down, raked over the ashes and added some logs and a few lumps of coal. Within a few moments reviving flames licked the coal and the logs crackled into life. The warm scent of applewood filled the room. Judith crouched and warmed her hands against the flames.

'That's better. Thank you, Angela. You always know how to act in a crisis.'

'Is being cold a crisis?' she asked.

'I come from a warm-blooded climate so in my case, yes it is.' Judith stood up and placed an elegantly manicured hand on the mantelpiece. 'We need to talk.'

'We'd better wait for Russ,' Angela insisted.

'What I have to say won't take long; it is of a personal nature and something I would prefer not to have to say in front of Russ.'

Angela's heart thumped against her ribcage. She hoped Judith wasn't going to make a scene.

'If it's about what happened in the bay . . . '

'It's about you and Russ.'

'Russ and I are not romantically involved,' Angela began.

'That is not true. My mother saw it from the beginning and in matters of this nature she is never wrong.'

'There is nothing between us,' Angela insisted.

'Whether you want there to be or not, there is. I'm French. Like my mother, I know about these things. You are in love with Russ. I can see it in your eyes and in his way he is equally mad about you. It was silly of me to think otherwise or to try to change things. It is the course of nature.'

'How long have you had these

suspicions?' Angela asked.

'From the moment I first saw you together. Why else do you think I treated you so badly? I was jealous.' Judith looked at Angela as if expecting her to say something, but when she didn't, she carried on. 'And I could see my son was mad about you too. That's not an easy thing for a mother to take. I nurtured the faint idea that Russ and I might get back together again, but I realise now that is not possible. Although I shall always admire and respect Russ, our lives are destined to go in different directions.'

'Were you really going to run away with Jack tonight?' Angela asked.

'That's something else I said to annoy you,' Judith admitted. 'I was so mad I said the first silly thing that came into my head. I will admit I used him. I use all the men in my life. I can't help it.' She shrugged. 'But I do have one saving grace. I am a mother who loves her son and I would fight tooth and nail to stop any harm coming to him,' she said with a simple smile. 'You do believe me?'

'Yes, I do,' Angela replied, 'Mikey is a great credit to you. He's a happy well adjusted little boy who loves both his parents.'

'I have done some stupid things in my time but marrying Russ was not one of them. The stupid thing was letting him go. I hope you can understand that a part of me will always love Russ. He is the father of my child and as such will obviously have a place in my life.'

'Why are you telling me this?' Angela asked.

'Because you will be taking my place of course. At least I hope you will. I am happy that Mikey loves you and I know he will be in good hands.'

'You're definitely not taking him back to Paris?'

For a second there was the suggestion of a mischievous twinkle in Judith's eyes.

'To live off the proceeds of my inheritance you mean?'

Recalling what Jack had told her about the inheritance Angela did her best not to smile.

'Jack told you, didn't he?'

'You must have been so disappointed,' Angela sympathised, not wanting to make mileage out of the distressing incident.

'I was more than that, Angela. I was ver' angry, but now I have calmed down and I can see the funny side of it. My uncle and I never really got on and I think he did it as some sort of revenge. I was always playing tricks on him when my mother took us visiting. One time I put salt in the sugar bowl and another boot blacking on the bottom of his shoes. There was such a mess. As a bachelor my uncle did not take kindly to having his orderly life interrupted by a nuisance of a child. Eventually he got his own back by leaving me that dreadful well.' She made a disgusted noise at the back of her throat. 'You should have seen the thing. The smell was indescribable. I shall never visit it again. As far as I am concerned they can board it over and throw away the key if there is one. If it turns into an oil well, then and only then will I be interested. So now you know the full story.'

'If you won't be going back to the château will you be going back to France?' Angela asked.

'I have to and the sooner the better. My life is in Paris and I have the promise of an interview for a new job. I must get a job if I am to live so yes I will be going back. I believe it was you who once pointed out to me that Paris is not very far away and that if my son stayed in this country I could see him as often as I would like?'

'That remark came out all wrong.'

'Like a lot of things it doesn't matter now. What does matter is that we become friends. Do you think that would be possible?'

Angela looked at Judith and wondered how many more surprises there were in store for her tonight.

'I'll admit I was making plans to

271

leave England with Mikey but not with Jack. When that wretched mechanic of his didn't turn up as arranged I began to have second thoughts. In Paris I would have had no help looking after my son. Here he has an army of people eager to look after him, so much so I fear he may be spoilt. It is much better for him to stay here.'

'Friends it is,' Angela agreed.

'Then we must seal it with a kiss.'

Judith embraced her on both cheeks. A movement in the doorway drew her attention away from Angela.

'There you are,' she greeted Russ with a warm smile. 'Angela and I are all finished up here, so I will leave you to go and say good night to Mikey. If you hear raised voices it will be me having stern words with my mother-in-law about picnics on dangerous beaches.'

She touched Russ gently on the cheek as she passed him.

'You need not worry that I will make a nuisance of myself,' she said.

The smell of French perfume lingered on the air after she left the room.

'What all that was about?' Russ demanded.

'I think,' Angela said slowly, 'that Judith has just given us her blessing.'

'For what?' Russ frowned.

'Our union.'

'Now you really have lost me.'

'I know a female is only supposed to do this sort of thing in a leap year, but I'm not prepared to waste any more time,' Angela said.

'To do what?'

'I have no intention of going down on one knee and if you turn me down tradition demands you buy me a silk dress, but to be honest I would rather have a new bicycle.'

'Are you feeling quite well, Angela?' Russ looked totally perplexed.

'Here goes.' Angela took a deep breath.

'What are you going to do?' There was a look of alarm on his face now.

'I would be honoured if you would

consent to be the husband of the new head teacher of St Andrew's — junior wing,' she added, 'so I'm asking you to marry me.'

'I see.' Russ's brow cleared.

'Well?' Angela prompted.

'My answer is no.'

18

'You're turning me down?' Angela took a step backwards.

'I am.'

'May I know why?'

'Whatever happened to, 'Quite frankly the idea is a bit of a laugh,' or words to that effect? I didn't mishear that day in the kitchen did I?' Russ enquired politely.

Angela flushed.

'I didn't want Judith causing trouble.'

'It wasn't true?' Russ persisted.

'I have just asked you to marry me. Look,' Angela reasoned, 'if you want to make me squirm go ahead. I feel silly enough as it is racing over here to warn you about her. She's not going anywhere by the way, at least not with Mikey, and not in the immediate future.'

'I'm pleased to hear it.'

'Judith likes the idea of us getting

275

married. Did I mention she's my new best friend?'

'What exactly were you and Judith talking about?'

'Amongst other things we were discussing you.'

'I thought my ears were burning.'

'Judith wants to move back to Paris.'

'I know.'

'Don't keep interrupting.'

'Sorry.'

'She is prepared to leave Mikey here if I am part of the deal.'

'She said that?'

'In not so many words.' Angela had the grace to blush. 'Actually what she said was she wanted to move on with her life and that she wouldn't be difficult if you and I, well, got it together?'

'What a charming turn of phrase.'

'So?'

'What about Jack Brewer?'

'He doesn't figure in the deal.'

'You went out to dinner with him this evening.'

'Yes,' Angela acknowledged slowly.

'Incidentally you haven't fully explained what are you doing here?'

'Jack told me he suspected Judith was planning to leave for France and quite soon. With Pauline in hospital and you being frequently away, now seemed an ideal time for her to leave and take Mikey with her. Jack said he would have told me on Monday but my foot hurt and I didn't go out to dinner with him. Monday is always a bad day anyway. Most restaurants are closed. Er, where was I?'

'I'm not too sure,' Russ murmured, 'we seem to have strayed off the topic.'

'I remember,' Angela battled on. 'Judith chatted up one of Jack's mechanics and he promised to give her a lift I think, I'm not really sure of the details on that, but he didn't turn up as planned. Sorry, don't know why. After Jack told me of his suspicions we drove over here to warn you what was in the wind and that's about it really.'

'Can I ask another question?'

'Fire away.'

'Are you in love with me?'

'I've been in love with you ever since we had that dance at your eighteenth birthday party,' Angela replied with a half smile, 'but I was a bit too young for that sort of thing then and we both had a lot of living to do. I suppose it's too much to expect you felt the same way?'

'I always thought of you as a bit of an annoying little pest, you and my sister that is. You were always following me around.'

'Do you still feel the same way about me?' Angela asked in a quiet voice.

'I haven't felt that way about you for a long time but you haven't exactly given me the green light.'

'How could I? There was Judith treating me like the hired help, then Jack being a nuisance, not to mention accidents all over the place, then everyone warning me off you.'

'What? Why?'

'It was pointed out to me that to get involved with you could be regarded as unprofessional as you are the father of one of my pupils, and if I wanted the job of head of school maybe I should cool it. So I did.'

'I had no idea so much drama was going on in the background.'

'You were busy with your boardroom furniture.'

'I still am,' Russ pointed out, 'though goodness knows when I'll get back to work.'

'Well I think I've said everything I wanted to say.'

'And you really are the new head of St Andrew's junior wing?'

'I heard earlier today that I've been successful in my application.'

'Then congratulations are in order I think.' Russ smiled.

'And that's the last of the complications out of the way, isn't it?' Angela enquired.

'It seems to be.'

'Would you reconsider your decision?'

'You do realise what you are letting

yourself in for should we get married?'

'A hyperactive five-year-old son; a French ex-wife; a rather demanding mother?' Angela counted them off on her fingers. 'Have I missed anything?'

'You haven't mentioned a workaholic carpenter who can at times be a bit grumpy.'

'I forgot that one,' Angela conceded.

'Is that how you see me?' Russ asked.

'Sometimes.' Angela moved away from the fire as the heat became too much for her. 'But I'm prepared to take the risk.'

Russ took a step towards her.

'I suggest we seal the deal with a kiss.'

His lips on hers were cold, but as his hand slipped around the back of her waist her body warmed to his touch. The firm wall of his chest against hers as he increased the pressure of the embrace was a solid support to her legs as Angela began to fear they might give way under her.

A loud thump from the room above

separated them with a jolt.

'Do you think that's my mother trying to gain our attention?' he asked with a resigned smile.

'It could be Mikey,' Angela replied. 'Why don't we go upstairs, find out what's going on and break our news?'

'Now?'

'There's no time like the present.'

'Then you've reconsidered? You accept my proposal?'

'With all my heart.'

Russ kissed her again before gently releasing her.

'Let's get going. Everyone's here and goodness knows when we'll be able to get them together again and in the mood to speak to each other in a reasonably civilised manner.'

'Judith did mention having words with your mother about picnics on the beach. I'm not sure how civilised that exchange would be.'

'I hope they'll stop arguing long enough to give us their congratulations.'

'Then anything you say.' Angela

linked her arm through Russ's.

'May I ask when you take up your new position?'

'September.'

'I promise to be on my best behaviour when you introduce me to everyone.'

'They know you already,' Angela said as they began to mount the stairs.

'They probably also know that you and I were engaged in somewhat unseemly activities while your job application was going through.'

'We weren't,' Angela protested.

'Sunset walks along the beach? Holding hands, paddling in the sea, kissing each other, eating chocolate eggs and sharing scones and jam?'

'I suppose it doesn't get much worse than that,' Angela agreed. 'I'm amazed they gave me the job.'

'Especially after Ma went and disgraced herself even further by being airlifted to hospital. You were never out of the news. In your position I'd have had nothing to do with our family.'

'Perhaps I should reconsider,' Angela teased.

'No way. I'm not letting Jack Brewer back in your life.'

'He and I are just good friends,' Angela insisted.

'Keep it that way,' Russ said as they reached the top of the stairs. 'Now how shall we do this?'

There was a hurried scuffle behind Pauline's bedroom door.

Angela sighed. 'They've been eavesdropping.'

'In that case,' Russ raised his voice, 'Angela and I are getting married,' he announced, 'so for the next few weeks would you all please behave?'

The next moment the landing was full of people, one mobile stretcher and an entire ambulance crew, everyone anxious to offer their congratulations.

'I don't think my words had any effect on them whatsoever,' Russ complained with a look of resignation as kisses were exchanged and the decibel level grew dangerously high with everyone shouting at everyone else.

Mikey tugged at his father's jumper.

'What is it?' Russ demanded. 'I was just about to give Angela a kiss.'

'Do you think Angela would like a new football as a wedding present?' he asked hopefully.

THE END

GRACIE'S WAR

Elaine Everest

Britain is at war — but young Gracie Sayers and her best friend Peggy are determined they will still have fun, enjoying cinema trips and dances with Peggy's young man Colin and her cousin Joe. However, there is something shifty about Joe, and Gracie finds she much prefers Colin's friend, the kind and decent Tony. Then, one night, a terrible event changes everything. Now Tony is away at war — and Gracie is carrying the wrong man's child . . .

CUPCAKES AND CANDLESTICKS

Nora Fountain

When Maddy's husband Rob suddenly announces that he's leaving her and moving to Canada with his pretty young employee, her world comes crashing down. As Rob's promises of financial support prove worthless, Maddy finds herself under growing pressure to forge a new life for herself and her four children. She decides to start a catering business, but will it earn enough money — and is that what she really wants? And then she meets the gorgeous Guy in the strangest of circumstances . . .

FLIGHT OF THE HERON

Susan Udy

On her deathbed, Christie's mother confides to her daughter that she has family she never knew existed — grandparents, a great-aunt, and an uncle — and elicits a promise from Christie to travel to Devon to meet them. When she arrives, she's surprised to find another man living there: the leonine and captivating Lucas Grant. But when her grandmother decides to change her will and leave Christie a sizeable inheritance, it's soon all too evident that someone wants to get rid of her, and both her uncle and Lucas have a motive . . .

THE DAIRY

Chrissie Loveday

Georgia is the rebellious eldest daughter of George Wilkins, managing director of the family business, Wilkins' Dairy. Studying for a degree in art, she has become involved with a fellow student, Giles. Following lunch with him and his eccentric artist mother, she ends up moving in with them — but finds it hard adjusting to such a dramatically different lifestyle. Meanwhile, George is struggling with difficulties of his own at the dairy. Can father and daughter both deal with their troubles and find contentment?

A WHOLE NEW WORLD

Sheila Holroyd

Marla's attempts to become an actress and model have stalled. While she decides what to do next, she goes to live in her dead uncle's house in the country, with its tantalising clues to his mysterious past. Then comes an unexpected chance to restart her modelling career — but if she seizes this opportunity it will mean abandoning the new life she has made for herself, and not only new friends but also a possible romance. Which should she choose?